Michael Frayn was born in London in 1933 and began his career as a journalist on the *Guardian* and the *Observer*. His novels include *Headlong*, *Spies* and *Skios*. He has also published two works of philosophy, *Constructions* and *The Human Touch*, and a memoir, *My Father's Fortune*. His seventeen plays range from *Noises Off*, recently chosen as one of the nation's three favourite plays, to *Copenhagen*. He is married to the writer Claire Tomalin.

by the same author

fiction
THE RUSSIAN INTERPRETER
TOWARDS THE END OF THE MORNING
A VERY PRIVATE LIFE
SWEET DREAMS
THE TRICK OF IT
A LANDING ON THE SUN
NOW YOU KNOW
HEADLONG
SPIES
SKIOS

non-fiction
CONSTRUCTIONS
CELIA'S SECRET: AN INVESTIGATION (with David Burke)
THE HUMAN TOUCH
MY FATHER'S FORTUNE

plays
THE TWO OF US
ALPHABETICAL ORDER
DONKEYS' YEARS
CLOUDS
BALMORAL
MAKE AND BREAK
NOISES OFF
BENEFACTORS
LOOK LOOK
HERE
NOW YOU KNOW
COPENHAGEN
ALARMS & EXCURSIONS
DEMOCRACY
AFTERLIFE

films and television
CLOCKWISE
FIRST AND LAST
REMEMBER ME?

translations
THE SEAGULL (Chekhov)
UNCLE VANYA (Chekhov)
THREE SISTERS (Chekhov)
THE CHERRY ORCHARD (Chekhov)
THE SNEEZE (Chekhov)
WILD HONEY (Chekhov)
THE FRUITS OF ENLIGHTENMENT (Tolstoy)
EXCHANGE (Trifonov)
NUMBER ONE (Anouilh)

collections
COLLECTED COLUMNS
STAGE DIRECTIONS
TRAVELS WITH A TYPEWRITER
MATCHBOX THEATRE: THIRTY SHORT ENTERTAINMENTS

THE TIN MEN

Michael Frayn

FABER & FABER

First published in 1965 by William Collins Sons & Co. Ltd
Published in Penguin Books 1995

This paperback edition first published in 2015
by Faber & Faber Limited
Bloomsbury House, 74–77 Great Russell Street
London WC1B 3DA

Printed in the UK by CPI Group (UK) Ltd, Croydon, CR0 4YY

A CIP record for this book
is available from the British Library

ISBN 978–0–571–31589–5

My first novel, published exactly fifty years ago. Always something of a challenge for the young writer, that first novel. These days, judging by the number of courses you see advertised offering to teach you how to write one, it must be a rite of passage almost as common as the first date or the first driving lesson. A bit daunting still, all the same.

In my case, actually, I wasn't really so young – thirty-two, an age by which a lot of writers have written not only their first novel but their best – even their last – and are already sinking into obscurity, celebrity, or alcoholism. It had been hanging over me, like a mountain waiting to be climbed, for quite some time. But I'd been writing a humorous newspaper column three times a week, and it hadn't left me with much breath for the great ascent. So I'd moved to another newspaper, where I had to write only one column a week, and cleaned out the type on my type-writer once again.

Nor was it the first book I'd had published – there had already been two selections from the column. It wasn't even the first novel I'd *written*. That had been six years earlier, when I was still a reporter. I'd sent it to my newly acquired literary agent, who said she quite liked the first thirty pages, but not the three hundred that followed, which she advised me to put away in a dark place somewhere far from the eyes of man. I had at any rate the good sense to obey, and when I looked at the manuscript again a few years ago I realised that even her cautious approval of the first eleventh of the book had been recklessly soft-hearted.

One of the characters in the story that I now began is also struggling to write his first novel (a boldly original touch, it seemed to me at the time, but I've realised since that it's one quite a lot of first-time novelists resort to). His name is Hugh Rowe, but whether he is the hughrowe of only his own novel, or whether he's supposed to have some likeness to me, I'm not sure. His aims are actually rather higher than mine. He seems to be trying to imitate one or more of the accepted literary forms of the time, whereas I wasn't venturing all that far from what I'd been doing in my column, with its short takes, broad satire, and staff of simple comic characters.

I recall quite a lot of agonising even so, but I must in fact have done it fairly quickly, because the acceptance from the publishers – the first reference I can find to the book in my files – is dated only eighteen months (and seventy or so weekly columns) later. The advice of my then editor, Richard Ollard (himself a distinguished writer and historian), was pretty much the exact converse of my agent's about the earlier book – it was the first thirty or so pages that he didn't like. I was greatly cheered, of course, by this shift in the balance of approval, and was happy to accept his advice to consign those first thirty to the same oblivion as the previous three hundred and thirty.

He had a lot of other good suggestions, too, and I was touched to see, when I looked up the subsequent correspondence in my files just now, that in his letters there are also many comments added in another hand – the early scribblings of my eldest daughter, then aged two, now long since a novelist and screenwriter herself.

So, 1965.

T. S. Eliot had died at the beginning of the year and Winston Churchill was just about to. The Beatles were conquering the world, and America was being slowly sucked into Vietnam. Somewhere beyond the headlines computers – the tin men of my title – were beginning to make their importance felt, if only by their ponderous size and cost. They were produced, mostly by IBM, for a small elite of academic and commercial users, and they were as imposing in their way as the great steam engines that had ushered in an earlier technological revolution. There's a picture on Wikipedia of an IBM 704 mainframe, dated 1964. It occupies an entire room – four steel cabinets as tall and voluminous as commercial refrigerators, together with a steel desk suite as imposing as the control room of an aircraft carrier. Amongst it all, easy to overlook surrounded by all that hardware, is a demure young woman in a pencil skirt who is presumably the operator. She seems as overawed as all the rest of us, and as unaware as IBM themselves that in forty or fifty years' time the balance of power would have been reversed, and she would be carrying the same capacity and more tucked away unnoticed inside the smartphone in her shirt pocket.

It was mighty IBM mainframes that I envisaged as the equipment of the William Morris Institute of Automation Research, where my story is set. The scale of the hardware seems to have overpowered the judgment of a lot of readers and reviewers, who thought it was the machines and their programmers that I was mocking, whereas I had supposed that my target was the professional people – the journalists, lawyers, clergymen, etc. – whose thinking was so stereotyped that it could be carried out just as effectively by a machine. I hadn't in those days heard of the Turing Test – Alan Turing's proposal that a computer could be said to think if its conversational powers were shown to be indistinguishable from a human being's – so I didn't realise that what I was suggesting was a kind of converse of it: a demotion of human beings to the status of machines if their intellectual performance was indistinguishable from a computer's, and they become tin men in their turn.

The William Morris Institute is about to be visited by the Queen for the opening of a new wing, and I realise with hindsight that I've used a similar idea quite often since: the grand event that goes wrong, and deposits the protagonists into the humiliating gulf that so often in life opens between intention and achievement. My characters at the Institute could have written a story programme for me and saved me a lot of work. I've become a bit of a tin man myself.

One of the consequences of reaching the skyline of that first mountain, of course, was the sight of yet another mountain rising beyond – the second novel. It also brought me the Somerset Maugham Award, a travel grant set up by Maugham to encourage writers in the early stages of their careers. In those days it was worth £500, and you had to promise to stay out of the country for three months, 'with the object of acquainting yourself with the manners and customs of foreign nations'. Maugham probably saw the likely recipient as a young bachelor, and as spending his exile in some low-wage economy in the Far East where he could have a comfortable life and a few poignant sexual adventures of one sort or another without going beyond his budget. I was married, though, with two small children, and we spent our exile *en famille* in the United States, so for me it was an expensive benefaction to receive, and offered little opportunity for adventures.

We did find out a bit about local manners and customs, though. One of them was the engaging readiness with which the most ordinary people in the States, not just adventuresses after your winnings in the casino, came up to you on trains and even in the street and told you their life stories in the most intimate detail. "Hey, I love kids!" said an elderly gentleman who happened to be passing somewhere in mid-town Manhattan, at the sight of ours. "I've just cut my only son out of my will." The children themselves (now a little older, and no longer scribbling their comments on my literary archive) made another discovery. Looking upwards at the world from their viewpoint so close to the floor they found an aspect of America that many visitors probably miss – the underside of luncheon counters, which are all decorated with a varicoloured impasto of dried chewing gum as impressive in its way as the ceiling of the Sistine Chapel.

The book also led to two of the Meetings with Famous Men that make the later stages of a writer's memoirs so much less enjoyable to read about than the Early Struggles. The first was with J. B. Priestley, by then in his seventies, but still perhaps the most successful British writer alive. He summoned me to his impressive country house near Stratford-on-Avon and announced that he wanted to turn my novel into a play. I was flattered, of course, and intrigued. He had recently had a considerable hit with the

viii

adaptation that he and Iris Murdoch had made of her novel *A Severed Head*. I was rather dubious, though, as we talked about it, whether he and I, or he alone, or even both of us in concert with Shakespeare and Chekhov, could achieve the same results with mine. The slightness of the characters and plot, and the literary nature of so much of the humour, seemed to me ill-suited for drama. He was a strong-minded man, and he brushed my objections aside like so much fluff. He knew a great deal about the theatre, he said, and I knew nothing. Which I had to admit was true, and I reluctantly agreed to allow him to do a sample first act.

It arrived only a week or so later. I was immediately impressed by the typing, which was flawless and most beautifully formatted, with the dialogue in black and the stage directions in red – something I had never seen before and never have since. What was typed, though, whether in red or in black, justified all my worst fears. I summoned up my courage and wrote the most tactful letter I could, aborting the whole enterprise and returning his elegant typescript.

It was elegant no longer, I discovered. I had put it on the floor beside my desk while I concentrated on the politeness of my refusal, and my second daughter, aged one, now long since employed in the worlds of broadcasting and publishing, had made her entrance upon the literary stage like her sister before her, not this time by scribbling her comments on the text, but by ripping the pages out of the file one by one, tearing them up, and attempting to eat them. I agreed with her judgment, but I was embarrassed at the frankness with which she had expressed it. I parcelled up the resultant mess as best I could, and added an even more grovelling postscript to my letter. Priestley behaved with the utmost grace, I have to record, both about my rejection of his helping hand and my daughter's loyal and only too eloquent support for me.

My second meeting, which particularly delighted me because I was a great admirer, was with Kurt Vonnegut. He had reviewed the book in *Life* magazine, and then, in 1971, when he set up his own film production company on the proceeds from the success of *Slaughterhouse-Five*, bought the film rights. (He called the company Sourdough, after the old prospectors in the Yukon, because, as he assured me, there was gold in them thar hills.) I went to New York to stay with him and discuss how we were going to do it. I had a delightful few days walking through the baking July streets with him while he recalled bits of the book that had particularly amused him. He was a man who was easily amused, and laughter welled out of him like foam from champagne. He was also a heavy smoker, so that every time he laughed not only did the tears run down his cheeks but he would have to stop in the middle of the sidewalk and double up, coughing and choking, unable to breathe. Several times I feared that his new vocation as movie producer was going to finish him off somewhere along Third Avenue. We couldn't think of how to make a film out of the material, though, any more than Priestley could a play, and the gold remained, like most of the gold sought by prospectors in the film business, concealed where it was in those tantalising hills.

But at least none of my children offered their assistance, and Kurt and I remained friends for many years. Even after we had lost touch towards the end of his life he evidently retained his regard for the book, and in an interview he gave in those last years, where he was talking about the growing difficulties of writing comedy as one got older, I was surprised to read that after *The Tin Men* I had never been able to write anything funny again. Since he had later come to the first night of *Noises Off* on Broadway I took this as a considerable testimony to the consistency of his opinions.

Successive publishers in London have kept the book in print, but in America, in spite of Kurt's support, it has long since vanished. Now, fifty years after the whole adventure started, not to mention ten more novels and sixteen plays, here it comes again – my first published novel, and also, or so Kurt insisted, my last laugh.

MICHAEL FRAYN

"Breadth of vision" was a peculiarity much recommended at Amalgamated Television, and from the Chairman's suite in the penthouse on top of Amalgatel House the vision was as broad in every direction as the industrial haze would allow. At the windows of the suite linen slub curtains for ever sunlit by concealed spotlights stirred endlessly in a gentle summer breeze blown by concealed fans, warmed by concealed heaters, and made country fresh by concealed air-conditioners. They brushed with disarming simplicity against low afrormosia benches, on which tropical plants grew, perpetually watered by invisible built-in moisturising systems. On the walls there hung pictures by Pollock, Riopelle, de Staël, Rothko, and the Chairman's nephew; and in the outer office there sat two Programme Controllers, one Co-ordinating Producer, two Visualisation Directors, and three Programme Co-ordination Visualisers, who had been summoned for an urgent conference with the Chairman two and a half hours previously, and who had been sitting waiting ever since, at a total labour cost to the Chairman and his fellow shareholders of £24 an hour.

The Chairman was in conference. The fact was announced all over Amalgatel House on little lighted screens. "R.V. in conference," they glowed, wherever men's heads might be lifted up to appreciate the news, in lobby, garage, and canteen. One shone in the Chairman's waiting-room, for the benefit of the assembled surtax payers. The Chairman's secretary emerged from her office and examined them all for the sixth time with a certain suppressed satisfaction.

"I'll go in again and remind R.V. you're here," she said kindly.

She knocked softly on the Chairman's door and went in.

Rothermere Vulgurian was striding slowly round the room, his hands behind his back, the summer sunlight from the windows glinting softly on his distinguished silver hair.

"R.V.," she said. Without looking at her, Mr. Vulgurian detached a hand from behind his back and waved her out of the room. He was in conference with Sir Prestwick Wining, a working member of the Amalgamated Television Board who was responsible for the public, human and cultural relations side. Sir Prestwick, a small, sad, inert man, sat in a deeply-padded swivel chair in the middle of the room, turning slowly round and round like a sunflower to keep his face towards the Chairman.

Mr. Vulgurian stopped to pick absent-mindedly at the impasto on a Pollock.

"And another thing," he said. "Who's producing 'It's a Giggle' now?"

"Corbishley," said Sir Prestwick.

"Ah. I want you to go to our friend Corbishley and tell him that Lord Wastwater went on that programme last night with his tie under one ear."

"I'll tell him, R.V."

"Make it clear to him that I'm not criticising the technical or artistic side of the show."

"Not the technical or artistic side."

"I don't pretend to be competent to criticise that side of our shows. Never have, and don't suppose I ever will. I know my limitations, Prestwick. I employ experts to tell me whether our shows are competitive from the technical, artistic, and moral standpoint. I have full confidence in them. Tell Corbishley that."

"I will, R.V."

"But I do know when I see a man with his tie under one ear, or a girl with her shoulder strap coming down. And I won't have it on one of our shows."

"I agree entirely, R.V."

"I've an eye for detail, Prestwick, an eye for detail."

"You certainly have, R.V."

"I don't pretend to be an expert on television. I don't pretend to know very much about business or money. But I do claim to have an eye for detail."

"An eye for detail."

"It's the secret of successful management, Prestwick. Look after the small things, and the big things will look after themselves."

"Look after themselves. Exactly."

"I think the staff respect it too, don't they?"

"Of course they do, R.V."

"I think they do. I think they do."

Mr. Vulgurian stopped and smoothed down his fine silver hair. It aided his thinking, and he believed in thinking. Once he had said to Sir Prestwick, "If I were asked to put my advice to a young man in one word, Prestwick, do you know what that word would be?"

"No?" Sir Prestwick had said.

" 'Think,' Prestwick, 'Think.' "

"I don't know, R.V. 'Detail?' "

"No, Prestwick, 'Think' "

"Er. 'Courage?' "

"No. 'Think.' "

"I give up, R.V. 'Boldness?' "

"For heaven's sake, Prestwick, what is the matter with you? 'Think!' "

" 'Integrity?' 'Loyalty?' 'Leadership?' "

" 'Think,' Prestwick! 'Think,' 'Think,' 'Think,' 'Think!' "

When had that been? Sir Prestwick's last duodenal crisis but one?

"Who's producing 'It's a Giggle' these days?" Mr. Vulgurian asked keenly.

"Corbishley, R.V."

"Ah, Corbishley. Well, tell him, will you, Prestwick?"

Sir Prestwick jotted down on his folder "Tell Corbishley," so that his complete notes on the subject under discussion now

3

read "Tell Corbishley. Tell Corbishley. Tell Corbishley." Sir Prestwick allowed a small sigh to slip furtively through his moustache. He was not a happy man. He had been appointed to the board of Amalgamated Television after being knighted for his services to British public relations, services which had consisted of being the only public relations man the knighting authorities could find who was not at that moment actually engaged in any morally offensive activity, since he was in hospital under an anæsthetic. For a start he had been responsible for the public relations side. But the public relations side had turned out to lead naturally into the cultural relations side, which meant being the relation between Mr. Vulgurian and culture, and the cultural relations side had opened imperceptibly into the human relations side, which involved being the relation between Mr. Vulgurian and all the human beings in the world apart from the public, who came under public relations. Sir Prestwick was visibly wasting away under the strain of the job.

"Another thing," said Mr. Vulgurian. "I counted five cigarette ends and four used matches on the floor of the lift this morning. What do you think of that?"

"Someone must have used a lighter, R.V.," said Sir Prestwick.

Mr. Vulgurian stopped in his tracks and inspected Sir Prestwick with an eye for detail.

"Tummy troubling you this morning, Prestwick?"

"Oh, well, you know, R.V. . . ."

"Tell me if you don't feel up to work. I can always struggle through on my own."

"I'm perfectly all right, R.V."

"Pour yourself a glass of Malvern water. Take a dry biscuit. Don't mind me."

Sir Prestwick jumped up and hastened across to the sideboard next to which Mr. Vulgurian was standing.

"Pour me a glass, too," said Mr. Vulgurian. "Where was I? Ah—five cigarette ends and four used matches in the lift. I want you to send a memorandum to all departments detailing what

I found and reminding everyone that the lifts are used by visitors to the building who may well base their impression of Amalgamated Television on what they find on the floor."

"What they find on the floor. I have that, R.V.," said Sir Prestwick, struggling to pour the Malvern water and take a note at the same time.

"Appeal to their better natures."

"I'll make a note of it, R.V."

"Wherever and whenever possible, Prestwick, we must appeal to the staff's better natures. They have them, if we have the confidence to trust in them. That's one of the fundamental principles of good management."

"Better natures—exactly."

"Always treat a man as you would wish to be treated yourself, be he the humblest doorman in the firm."

"Do as you would be done by."

"It's good human relations. It's good business. It's good ethics."

"It certainly is, R.V."

Mr. Vulgurian paused and stroked his hair, doing to it as he would be done by.

"Speaking of ethics," he said, "aren't we building a new ethics department for a theological college somewhere?"

"For an automation research institute," said Sir Prestwick, brightening up a little.

"Yes, something of that sort."

"I was hoping we'd have time to talk about that, R.V., because I've got some rather good news. They're getting the Queen to come down and open it."

"Really?"

"So I hear, R.V."

"Good, Prestwick, good. Very good. Pour yourself another glass of water."

Mr. Vulgurian reflected with a broad reflective vision.

"How did they manage it?" he asked.

"I don't know, R.V."

"I wonder how they managed it. I seem to remember you couldn't get us the Queen to open this place."

"No, I couldn't, R.V."

"And you couldn't get the Queen Mother, either."

"No."

"Nor Princess Alexandra."

"No."

"Nor the Duke of Kent."

"No."

"Nor the Duke of Gloucester."

"I got the Duke of Bedford, R.V."

"You got the Duke of Bedford."

Mr. Vulgurian took out his penknife and scraped abstractedly at a particularly protuberant knobule of pink paint on the Riopelle.

"How did they manage it, Prestwick? Are they able to pull strings? Is that it, Prestwick?"

"It's the Establishment, R.V. All these academics are hand in glove with the Establishment. They all hang together."

"The Establishment! Raising its ugly head again, eh? As you know, Prestwick, I don't pretend to have any political views—I have experts who look after that side of things for me. But it does seem to me symptomatic of something that a television organisation which provides the nation's main socio-cultural communications system cannot even get the Duke of Gloucester, while some little theological college catering for a tiny minority can get the Queen."

"Very true, R.V."

Mr. Vulgurian put the penknife back in his pocket and began to circle the room again.

"Then again," he said, "it is *our* wing that the Queen will be opening."

"That's true, too, R.V."

"You know, Prestwick, when I look into the future I am certain we are entering upon an era in which religion and mass communications will put all distrust and antagonism behind them, and learn to co-operate to their mutual advantage."

"That's certainly a thought, R.V."

"Jot it down, Prestwick, for my speech to the Association for the Furtherance of Responsible Television next week."

"I have, R.V. It's incorporated in the text of the speech I gave you yesterday."

"Good, Prestwick, good. It certainly bears out my point about the value of ethics. This little theological college ... Did you say it was a theological college, Prestwick?"

"A research establishment, R.V."

"This little research establishment came to us for help. We did not ask whether it was Protestant, Catholic, or Jewish. Did we ask, Prestwick?"

"Well, no, R.V., because it's ..."

"Because it's not our way. Without regard to colour, race, or creed, we gave what help we could."

"Fifty thousand pounds, R.V."

"Fifty thousand pounds."

Mr. Vulgurian completed three laps of the room in a reflective silence. Sir Prestwick was beginning to feel sick and dizzy with the constant revolving of the swivel chair.

"Fifty thousand pounds," said Mr. Vulgurian. "Fifty thousand pounds ... That figure was authorised by the board, wasn't it, Prestwick? Yes? But we have work to do. What work do we have to do, Prestwick?"

"I think you wanted to discuss the withdrawal of the 'Think Big' notices in all the executives' offices, R.V."

"Ah. We decided they were a little unsophisticated for an organisation like ours, didn't we?"

"I think we did, R.V."

"One of your less happy inspirations, Prestwick, though as you know, I never interfere in your running of the cultural side. What have you managed to cook up for us instead?"

"I wondered how you would feel about 'Only connect'?"

Mr. Vulgurian's secretary tiptoed into the room. He waved

her out again, and stopped, absorbed, in front of the Rothko, licking his finger and rubbing it against a mark on the canvas to find out whether it was paint or dirt.

"I know what I meant to ask you," he said. "Who's producing 'It's a Giggle' these days?"

2

The whole of the William Morris Institute of Automation Research rang with the bongling and goingling of steel scaffolding poles being thrown down from a great height. The new Ethics Wing was almost finished. It was not before time. The noise and other inconveniences caused by the building of it had considerably reduced the amount of automation the Institute had researched into during the past two years. Experts had calculated that if the revolutionary new computer programmes being designed at the Institute had gone ahead without interruption, they should have put some two million professional men out of work over the course of the next ten years. Now there was a risk that some of these two million would still find themselves in work, or at any rate only partly out of work. But then, said the optimists, for progress to be made someone always had to suffer.

Dr. Goldwasser, the Head of the Newspaper Department, was suffering already. Each fresh bongle or goingle made him jump, and each time he jumped he became more irritated. He didn't want his staff to see him jumping, in case they thought he had weak nerves. On the other hand, he didn't want them to see him making a fourth trip within three hours to the lavatory, where it was quiet, in case they thought he had a weak bladder.

He looked restlessly out of the window, to see if he could see how other people were coping. The only other person he could see was Rowe, the Head of the Sport Department, in his laboratory on the other side of the courtyard. Rowe seemed to be absorbed, which probably meant he was at work not on the automation of sport, but on the novel he was said to be writing. He alternately bent over his desk, pulling locks of hair over his eyes, and gazed vacantly out of his window, screwing his little finger around inside his right ear. At intervals he removed the finger and inspected it absently, as if he hoped he might have brought up traces of oil or uranium ore. Goldwasser was rather impressed by the spectacle of creation actually taking place, and after a bit found himself screwing his little finger around inside his right ear in sympathy.

He wondered if he should go along and drop in for a chat with Rowe. It could be quite strengthening. Rowe was certainly less clever than himself, and it had come to the point, Goldwasser tacitly admitted, where he found it definitely helpful to his morale to talk to people he was absolutely sure were less clever than he was. Not stupid people, to whom he was unable to say anything at all, but to clever people who were just not quite clever enough to be challenging. It left a wide field of potential comforters—almost everyone in the institute except Macintosh, the Head of the Ethics Department.

Agh! Macintosh! He was Goldwasser's closest friend, and the very thought of him filled Goldwasser with a warm, familiar irritation. He irritated Goldwasser in two ways—sometimes by seeming to be too stupid to talk to, and sometimes by seeming to be possibly cleverer than Goldwasser. Even more irritating than either state was the ambiguity of fluctuating between the two.

Was Macintosh cleverer than him or wasn't he? There must have been some objective way of telling. Once, he was sure, he had been indubitably cleverer than Macintosh. But he was slowing down. At least, he was afraid he was slowing down. He was pretty certain his brain was of the genus *Cerebrum Dialectici*—a logician's or child prodigy's brain, an early-flowering plant already past its best by the age of thirty. His anxiety on the point had developed into a sort of cerebral hypochondria. He was for ever checking his mental performance for symptoms of decline. He borrowed sets of IQ tests from his colleagues, and timed his performances, plotting the results on graphs. When he produced a graph with a curve that went downwards, he assured himself that it was merely a misleading technique; and when he produced one with a curve that went upwards, he told himself sceptically that it must be the result of experimental error.

One symptom of decay, he sometimes thought, was the loss of his opinions. Some people have faith; some people have opinions. Goldwasser had had opinions about almost everything he had ever heard of, and from the age of fourteen he had heard of almost everything in the universe. In the high summer of his cerebellum he had had the whole of creation divided into two great categories, the things he was for and the things he was against. Now his opinions were falling out like old teeth. His immediate circle of interest had shrunk from the fate of the pi-meson and the theocracy of the gods F and M to an intense consideration of whether or not he was cleverer than Macintosh.

Goldwasser could not see Macintosh out of the window, since he was hidden inside the Gothic fortress of the old Ethics Department, but the noise of the scaffolding being shed from Macintosh's new wing kept him constantly before Goldwasser's mind. *Was* Macintosh the cleverer? Was Macintosh's brain, like his, *Cerebrum Dialectici*? If it was, it was now at the very height of its powers and would subsequently decline at the same rate as his own, if indeed his own was declining. Or was it *Cerebrum Senatoris*—a wise old man's brain, slowly maturing over the years? If that was what it was, it might have drawn level with Goldwasser's brain without implying any deterioration in Goldwasser's own performance. But then again, if it did incline towards *Cerebrum Senatoris* rather then *Cerebrum Dialectici* it would go on improving relative to Goldwasser's, which was not a very cheering prospect. Goldwasser gloomily agitated his finger in his right ear. The ear had now begun to itch with a definite itch of its own.

Goldwasser suddenly realised he was being watched, and caught a pair of eyes gazing intently at him from well back inside a nearby corridor window. They belonged to Nunn, the Deputy-Director of the Institute. Nunn smiled cheerily, and gave a little wave. Goldwasser started nervously back into the room. He pulled the finger hastily out of his ear, then put it back as if he had intended to have it there all the while for some serious scientific purpose, and began to mess around with the papers on his desk.

Perhaps he would go for another pee after all.

There was no one in the Heads of Departments washroom when he got there except Jellicoe, the head porter. Jellicoe was leaning across a handbasin with his face very close to the mirror, trimming his moustache with a tiny pair of folding scissors. He glanced up at Goldwasser.

"Hallo, Mr. Goldwasser," he said, returning to his moustache.

"Hallo," said Goldwasser, who was never able to decide whether to call the porter Jellicoe or Mr. Jellicoe. He peed, then filled a wash-basin with luxurious quantities of hot water and washed his hands. It was very peaceful in the washroom, the deep calm emphasised by the periodic flushing of the cisterns, and the tiny snip-snip of Jellicoe's moustache-scissors.

"I see Dr. Riddle's published another paper on random distribution," said Jellicoe, his mouth somewhat constricted by the operations on his upper lip.

"Ah," said Goldwasser, gazing at himself in the mirror. In general terms he could not doubt that he was clever; too clever, even—too clever by half, if not by three-quarters.

"Have you read it, sir?" asked Jellicoe.

"No," said Goldwasser. The only way he could read a newspaper, let alone a learned article, was back to front, from bottom to top of the page, from tailpiece to headline, setting himself and solving outrageous problems of comprehension in every paragraph. On days of unusual greyness he deliberately increased the masochistic pleasure of the perversion by reading each sentence back to front as well.

"A rather brilliant piece of work," said Jellicoe. "Or so I thought."

Goldwasser looked at strip cartoons backwards, too, divining with depressing accuracy what was going to be in the first frame before he got back to it, bored by the logical impossibility of taking each single picture backwards.

"I hear from a rather reliable source," said Jellicoe, "that the Queen is coming down here."

"Oh?" said Goldwasser. He also read novels back to front. He could not bear the thought, when he picked up a novel, of suffering the author's tedious assumption in the early chapters that he knew nothing about the characters and would have to be introduced to them.

"To pay an official visit to the Institute and open the new wing. What do you think of that, sir?"

"Hm," said Goldwasser. There was just a chance that he might be able to face being introduced to a novelist's characters after he had discovered whether they finished up dead, married, or resigned to life. But then there wasn't much interest in learning that someone you knew nothing about was dead, married, or resigned to anything.

"I think myself," said Jellicoe, "that in some sense it marks the coming of age of automation research. We are being received into the body academic."

On the whole, thought Goldwasser, he preferred the television, where they showed you everything the right way round by *force majeure*, and made no concessions to the aberrant tastes of people like himself, who were too clever to know what was good for them. He dried his hands thoughtfully.

Outside the washroom door Nunn, the Deputy-Director, a squash racket under his arm, stood bent with his ear at the keyhole. He would not have Heads of Departments inviting other ranks into the washroom. It weakened discipline, and suggested the possibility of much more serious offences. Goldwasser again, of course. He looked in his Rugby Enthusiast's diary. It was the fourth trip to the washroom Goldwasser had made this morning. It was only Jellicoe's first visit, but he had been in there for nearly twenty minutes now.

Nunn was particularly pleased with the results of his spell at the washroom keyhole. It proved his contention that routine intelligence work often brought unexpected bonuses. If he hadn't been listening to hear why Goldwasser was associating with other ranks, he wouldn't have heard that the Queen was going to visit the Institute. That was a very valuable piece of information for the Institute's authorities to have. He made a note in the diary under Size in Gloves. "Queen," he wrote, and turned back to the Last Train section, in which Goldwasser's activities were noted. "Goldwasser," he wrote.

Goldwasser came out of the washroom. Nunn quickly straightened up.

"Jolly good," he said, chuckling and squeezing Goldwasser's arm. Then he walked noiselessly away up the corridor in his rubber badminton shoes.

3

"Hugh Rowe," wrote Hugh Rowe, "is a brilliant new arrival on the literary scene. *R* is his first novel, and critics who have seen it prior to publication have hailed the author as 'the most exciting new voice to become audible since the war,' and 'a dazzling new discovery who has achieved the staggering feat of uniting the sober density of Robbe-Grillet to the broad comic tradition of P. G. Wodehouse' (for full list see back flap)."

Rowe stopped, and revolved his finger in his ear. Writing a novel was astonishingly hard work. He had reached this point a dozen times—the desk and floor were littered with rejected drafts—and he was finding it very difficult to get beyond it. He tried again.

"*R* is the story of a whisky priest, tortured by the consciousness of having committed every sin, from blasphemy to murder, who is appalled by the ease with which he returns time and time again—as he knows with a deep inner conviction—to a state of grace."

Rowe winced and pulled the sheet out of the typewriter. He started again.

"*R* is the story of four men—a refugee dictator, an advertising copywriter, an alcoholic war-hero, and a class-conscious trade unionist—who find themselves marooned on a tiny island in the steaming heat of the Torres Strait. With them is a beautiful young society woman who was on her way to enter a nunnery . . ."

Rowe changed the paper.

"*R* is the odyssey of a disillusioned writer who moves through a series of fantastic adventures—each offering a devastating satire of a different aspect of our society—in his search for

R, a nebulous goal which is sometimes a city, sometimes a drug, sometimes a woman . . ."

Rowe sighed, and gazed out into the courtyard. Goldwasser had disappeared from his window. He had been visible for quite a long time, picking at his ear. Extraordinarily unappealing habits some people had. Rowe sighed again, energetically screwed his finger about in his ear, and wound a fresh sheet of paper into the typewriter.

"*R* is the story of a young man on his way up, who is determined to let nothing stand between him and the blonde in the E-type Jaguar . . ."

Rowe groaned. God in heaven, perhaps it *was* easier to write the book first and the jacket afterwards, after all. He wondered which way round other writers did it.

Still, the first paragraph was quite good. "Exciting new voice"—that was a pretty striking phrase. It made him feel rather exalted, and yet at the same time strangely humbled, to think that his virtues and talents had been charted with such accuracy, with such a downright willingness to give praise where praise was due.

The book was undoubtedly under way. That was the main thing. He put the various drafts away carefully, so that it would be possible later to follow the evolution of the passage and the development of his thinking, and began to automate a little sport.

4

Inside the old Ethics Department building, bright, wavering reflections danced over the walls, and small unseen impacts re-echoed with dreamlike magnitude. The door swung to behind Goldwasser with a noise like a howitzer going off. Goldwasser winced. Macintosh looked round and nodded at him. He was in his favourite position for ethical research, up on his gantry like the master of a ship on his bridge. He was leaning patiently and impassively on the rail, his great red face expressionless.

"Come on up," he called to Goldwasser, and the words lingered in the air impressively, as if they were written there.

Goldwasser climbed the steel ladder. The gantry spanned Macintosh's test tank. Macintosh had stripped everything out of his department—furniture, walls, floors—and sunk the test tank for his ethical machines. He was a single-minded man.

"We're just doing the last experiment of the run," said Macintosh. Goldwasser said nothing. He always felt rather uneasy about the test tank. It reminded him of the swimming baths, and made him feel defensive about his lack of muscles. At any moment he expected a gang of powerfully-built lower-class extroverts to pounce on him and throw him in. A girl at the far end of the tank giggled quietly at something; it echoed about the building as divine laughter, almost certainly directed at him.

The test tank occasionally reminded Macintosh of the swimming baths, too. In the summer he had once or twice dived in off the gantry fully-dressed, and swum an antique trudgeon up and down, pursued by his staff's respectable jokes. He did it to demonstrate to himself his spontaneity and casual disregard of convention, and because he had a complete change of clothes in the locker room, and also because a bellyflop stung much less if you were wearing a suit.

"Launch her," called Macintosh. A crane on the gantry swung a raft out over the water and started to lower it. On the raft, gazing at each other sombrely, sat Macintosh's Principal Research Assistant, Sinson, wearing an inflated yellow life-jacket, and his ethical machine, Samaritan II. A great echoing silence fell over the tank.

Macintosh had concentrated all his department's efforts on the Samaritan programme. The simplest and purest form of the ethical situation, as he saw it, was the one in which two people were aboard a raft which would support only one of them, and he was trying to build a machine which would offer a coherent ethical behaviour pattern under these circumstances. It was not easy. His first attempt, Samaritan I, had pushed itself overboard with great alacrity, but it had gone overboard to save anything which happened to be next to it on the raft, from seven stone of lima beans to twelve stone of wet seaweed. After many weeks of stubborn argument, Macintosh had conceded that the lack of discrimination in this response was unsatisfactory, and he had abandoned Samaritan I and developed Samaritan II, which would sacrifice itself only for an organism at least as compli-cated as itself.

The raft stopped, revolving slowly, a few inches above the water.

"Drop it," cried Macintosh.

The raft hit the water with a sharp report. Sinson and Samaritan sat perfectly still. Gradually the raft settled in the water, until a thin tide began to wash over the top of it. At once Samaritan leaned forward and seized Sinson's head. In four neat movements it measured the size of his skull, then paused, computing. Then, with a decisive click, it rolled sideways off the raft and sank without hesitation to the bottom of the tank.

"Save it, Lord," boomed Macintosh to a young man waiting on the side of the tank in a swimming costume. Lord dived in and attached a rope to the sunken Samaritan.

"Why don't you tie the rope to it before it goes overboard?" asked Goldwasser.

"I don't want it to know that it's going to be saved. It would invalidate its decision to sacrifice itself."

"But how would it know?"

"Oh, these Samaritan IIs are canny little beggars. Sometimes I think they understand every damned word you say to them."

"They're far too simple, Macintosh . . ."

"No, no. They come to trust you. So every now and then I leave one of them in instead of fishing it out. To show the others I mean business. I've written off two this week."

Samaritan was being hauled out on to the side of the tank, and held upside down to drain the water out of its works. Every now and then it ticked faintly, and shuddered.

"You've heard the news about your new wing, have you?" said Goldwasser.

"What news?"

"About the Queen."

"No?"

"She's coming down to open it."

"Really?"

He leaned over the rail and shouted: "Oh, Lord! Is it all right? Load it up for the next run, then."

"What are you doing now?" said Goldwasser.

"We're starting a new series to test its behaviour with simpler organisms."

Samaritan II came back up to the gantry, winched by the crane. There was something about its visible dials and displays that struck Goldwasser.

"Doesn't it look a bit sanctimonious to you?" he asked Macintosh.

"Aye, it always does after it's gone over the side. It's a minor defect. We'll get it right in development."

"But Macintosh, if it *enjoys* sacrificing itself it's not taking an ethical decision at all, is it?"

"I don't see why it shouldn't enjoy doing right."

"But if it's enjoyable it's not self-sacrifice."

19

"By God, Goldwasser, you're a real puritan! If a thing's right it's right, and if you enjoy doing it so much the better."

"It may be right. But for God's sake, Macintosh, it's not ethically interesting!"

They glared at one another in exasperation. It infuriated Goldwasser to think that this stubborn, slow-witted lump might in certain important ways be more intelligent than he was. He supposed that Macintosh must be no less irritated to think that in the long run his sound, slow-moving brains might not be competitive with Goldwasser's more flashy mental equipment.

"Anyway," he said, "the Queen's coming down to open your new wing."

"I suppose that's Nunn pulling strings again?"

"I suppose so."

"The Establishment at work once more."

"I suppose it means you'll have to install some experiments in it after all."

"It means nothing of the kind."

"You're still going to boycott it?"

"Certainly. I've told you. I've told Nunn. I'll have nothing to do with the new wing. I've no use for it. I'm too busy with the Samaritan programme. I've told them all along."

"There'll be trouble."

"Let there be."

A large sandbag was winched up to the gantry, and placed side by side with the Samaritan on the raft.

"Launch her!" shouted Macintosh.

The raft swung out over the water, and was lowered steadily away. The resonant silence fell once more.

"There's a logical flaw here," said Goldwasser suddenly, and his voice boomed about the roof.

"Drop her!" shouted Macintosh.

The noise of the raft hitting the water joined the reverberations of "There's a logical flaw here" and "Drop her!" on their complex journeys between wall and wall and tank and ceiling. Samaritan and the sandbag looked at one another impassively as the raft settled. When the deck was awash Samaritan seized the sandbag and attempted to measure the size of its skull. It attempted its four neat movements, frustrated by the un-skull-like shape of the sack, then paused, drew its conclusions, uttered a thoughtful whirr, and became completely still.

"Good lad," said Macintosh under his breath.

The deck of the raft was now completely submerged. Gradually the water rose around Samaritan and the sandbag as they sat stoically accepting their fate. The sandbag was the first to disappear. Then, with a last look of silent martyrdom, Samaritan vanished too. The bulging, shrinking, dark, refracted shape beneath the water went steadily down to the bottom.

"Well, I hope that meets all your objections to Samaritan I," said Macintosh. "You see it didn't even attempt to sacrifice itself for the sandbag."

"I see that," said Goldwasser. "But Macintosh, the only result was that they *both* went to the bottom."

"Oh, Goldwasser," said Macintosh, "you're just a rotten cynic."

5

Nunn put the squash racket he had been flexing down on his desk. He took the opportunity of being at the desk to look up the date of Henley. Then he selected a club from the golf bag in the corner of the office and began practising drives from a tee planted among the parched pile of the carpet.

Nunn was a reasonable man. He knew that the decision-making faculties of a professional decision-maker like himself had to be nursed. He therefore left all the routine work to his secretary, Miss Fram, and devoted his day to keeping fit. He kept fit with games. He followed a carefully planned schedule of playing games, preparing to play games, washing off the effects of playing games, watching other people play games, talking about playing games, and thinking about talking about playing games. While Miss Fram toiled in the outer office, revising superannuation schemes, engaging laboratory staff, and bargaining with union representatives about differentials in the Tea Room kitchen, Nunn oiled a cricket bat within, occasionally breaking off to ask Miss Fram to get him tickets for the police boxing championships, or to run round to the sports shop and fetch him another dozen shuttlecocks. That way he kept very fresh for when the really big decisions came along.

Anyway, games were important in another way. They gave him something to talk to his subordinates about. He was not, as he often pointed out, a computer man himself. He had spent most of his life as an army intelligence officer, stamping on the toes of obscure agitators in obscure territories, an activity which had given him a good practical grounding in human administration and man management. As an administrator, he found the subject of games was one you could talk to anybody about. He had talked about it to the private soldiers under his com-

22

mand. He had talked about it to the agitators he was interrogating, to set them at their ease before he stamped on their toes. He talked about it to all the Heads of Departments at the Institute. Tommies, darkies, longhaired intellectuals—they were all much of a muchness. Talk about games to them and they were all reduced to helpless silence.

He also talked about games to the Director, a practice which involved both the main axes of his life. Nunn put down his golf club and tiptoed across the carpet to a door in one corner which communicated with the Director's office. He bent down and looked through the keyhole. The Director was sitting at his desk—a large, awkward man sitting at a desk with a highly polished and completely empty top. Nunn peered at him with awe. The massive body was entirely immobile. The elbows were rested on the table, the fingers locked together, and the lips pursed against the thumbs, as if the Director was about to imitate the cry of an owl. The small, pale-blue eyes gazed out from the large head at a spot about three-quarters of the way along the surface of the desk, just short of the formal penholder. It was impossible to guess what prodigies of automational, philosophical, cybernetic, semantic, organisational, and indeed cosmological thought were taking place inside that massive head. He was clearly a man of heroic attributes, though their exact nature was lost in the sheer loftiness of the whole. Indeed, one of his few known attributes—and it required a definite mental effort to remember that he had *any*—was his name, which was Chiddingfold.

Nunn had a deep respect for Chiddingfold. When he was talking to the Heads of Departments he referred to him as Herr Direktor, or the Big White Chief, rather as some very religious people speak patronisingly of God and his friends, to show that they are so well in with that set that they no longer have to bother about sounding respectful. For the same reason Nunn spoke to Chiddingfold more or less as an equal. His merry chatter about broken collarbones, cracked knee-caps, and cut eyes was always listened to by Chiddingfold with a polite, uneasy smile. So was the cheerful office gossip with which Nunn also entertained the Director—speculations about whether Riddle was really a man, or whether Goldwasser was really a woman, or whether Haugh was really both at once. Nunn chuckled as he told it. But Chiddingfold just smiled uneasily, and his pale-blue eyes stared mildly at the middle of Nunn's chest.

Nunn did not make the heretical mistake of expecting Chiddingfold to *manifest* his power. He regarded himself as the man who really ran the Institute, who really took the decisions. But the power he wielded was only valid, he felt in the depths of his heart, because it descended through him from the taciturn godhead in the next office. Without the godhead there would have been no power to transmit, nor any authority to side with his subordinates against. It did not matter that Chiddingfold never said anything except "Good morning" and "Good afternoon." It would not have mattered if he had been totally dumb, or insane. It would not have mattered much if he had become invisible. The only thing that really mattered was that he was.

Nevertheless, Nunn would have liked to know more about what was going on inside Chiddingfold's huge head while the features on the front of it registered their minimal, obliging smile. It was a smile which was designed to fit on a man much smaller than Chiddingfold, and it left a great deal of room for manœuvre. Any thoughts thought by Chiddingfold would of course be immense, godly; but perhaps there was space among them for considerations inimical to cheery, simple, sporting Nunn. Nunn sometimes felt it would have been a relief if one afternoon those pale eyes had looked straight at him and Chiddingfold had said "Get stuffed, Nunn." At least he would have known where he stood. As it was he had to keep breaking off his schedule of games to do what he was doing now—to look through the keyhole of the communicating door to the Director's office, hoping to catch Chiddingfold in some act which betrayed his attitude towards him. But always Chiddingfold was doing the same thing. Always he was sitting at his desk, bulky and awkward, with his elbows resting on the polished, vacant desk-top, and his great head buttressed by his interlocked hands; motionless, cerebral, altogether too great for the limitations of human circumstance.

Nunn sighed noiselessly, afflicted with a certain respectful exasperation, and straightened up. He knocked on the door and went in.

"Good morning, Director," he said.

"Good morning," said Chiddingfold, lifting his head from his thumbs and stretching his lips in a minimal smile.

"New South Wales are 147 for 5. Heard it on the short wave half an hour ago. One of the Queensland slips has split his thumb rather nastily. Blood all over his flannels before they could get him off, I gather."

Chiddingfold's head sank back on to its mountings. His smile returned politely by way of acknowledgment, and went again.

"I don't know whether you've ever looked in the Heads of Departments bog, Director," Nunn went on, seating himself against the edge of an occasional table. "But some of these gentlemen are peeing four or five times in one morning. I may be a stuffy old soldier, but that seems a bit excessive to me, unless they've got notes from their doctors. Goldwasser's the worst offender.

"And another thing. The place is being used by ORs. They've got a perfectly good lavatory of their own, and they obviously wouldn't go in the Heads of Departments one if they weren't being encouraged. I'm pretty certain Goldwasser's inviting them in, as a matter of fact. Or at any rate he's not chucking them out, which comes to much the same thing. It's not the first time I've had occasion to take Goldwasser's name, either. We're going to have to keep our eye on that lad."

Nunn looked at Chiddingfold to see how he was reacting to this information. There was no sign of any reaction at all, so Nunn went on:

"Anyway, he can consider his name taken again."

Nunn inspected the toes of his shoes. He was trying to think

25

of a way of bringing up the question of the Queen's visit that wouldn't make him look ludicrously ill-informed if Chiddingfold had heard already.

"Now this business of the Queen's visit," he said at last.

The great head lifted off its hooks at once and looked straight at him, the pale blue eyes startled.

"Oh," said Nunn, "you hadn't heard, then, Director?"

The head moved minimally from side to side.

"Well, apparently the Queen's going to pay an official visit to the Institute and open the new wing."

The head relapsed slowly on to the thumbs. The eyes, however, looked not at the penholder but at the window. Chiddingfold was clearly excited by the news.

"So I'm told by my spies, anyway," said Nunn. "Nothing official yet, of course. One doesn't want to pontificate, but I myself—and this is merely my own personal opinion—feel that it in some sense marks the coming of age of automation research."

Chiddingfold looked up at Nunn for a moment.

"We are being received into the body academic," said Nunn. "To tell you the truth, Director, I thought you might have been pulling strings."

Chiddingfold allowed a disclaiming smile to shine palely for a moment.

"No?" said Nunn. "Well, it must have been Rothermere Vulgurian and his friends. What I believe is called the Establishment at work again. I suppose it has its uses in a case like this. Beats me how they do it. I suppose if you're as big as Vulgurian it just needs a word here and a word there. Money still talks, there's no getting away from it."

Chiddingfold's gaze seemed to be becoming very fixed on the penholder again. Nunn had a sense that the audience was drawing to a close.

"Jolly good," he said, consulting his watch. "If you'll excuse me, Director, I must slip away and get back to work. Lot on my plate to-day."

Chiddingfold nodded faintly and garnished the nod with the suggestion of a smile.

"Thank you," he said.

Nunn returned to his office and looked out his old football boots.

"Oh, Miss Fram," he said to his secretary in the outer office. "Be an angel and take these to the repairers before the shop shuts. I'm afraid I've got to dodge along now to some sheepdog trials."

"Very good, Mr. Nunn," said Miss Fram.

As Nunn hurried out, winking at her sportily and crying "Not a word to Bessy, mind," Miss Fram—angel, secretary, spinster, trump, treasure, and splendid little woman—thought an evil thought.

I think I'll take advantage of Mr. Nunn's absence, she thought. I'll just take his football boots to the repairer and adjudicate the window-cleaning tenders and initial the Tea Room accounts and work out which of the Heads of Departments ought to get rises next year and choose three guest lecturers for the extra-mural course and set up a committee to organise the Queen's visit, and then I'll go home early and take an aspirin, and see if I can shake this influenza off at last.

6

Rowe sat before his typewriter working on his novel. The particular problem he was grappling with was how to deflower the virginity of that first white page before him with such tact and passion that he would not spoil the delicate relationship between them for ever. He could almost see how to do it. There was a complete strategic plan inside his head. But the inside of his head also seemed to be full of water, and it was difficult to struggle near enough to see exactly how the plan started.

Suddenly he rushed at the page without inhibition.

"H," he wrote.

He looked at it. He was overcome with despair. He could scarcely have chosen a colder or less tactful letter to begin on. He ripped the paper out of the typewriter, wound in a fresh sheet, and pondered once more.

"H," he wrote suddenly.

What an appalling letter it was! It was a letter from which no sentence had ever set out on a successful journey in the whole history of literature. He changed the paper again.

"H," he wrote.

Was he mad? He crossed the soulless letter out and started yet again. "H," he typed. He crossed it out. "H," he typed. He crossed it out.

He sat back and screwed his finger about in his ear. Suddenly he became conscious that Goldwasser was watching him again out of the window of his laboratory. He took his finger out of his ear hastily and looked round. Goldwasser took *his* finger out of his ear, waved his hand, and darted nervously out of sight. Rowe started work again with a rush.

"Hugh Rowe," he wrote. Ah, that struck a chord!

"Was born," he wrote, "in Bromley, the son of a marine

insurance assessor. He was educated at Bromley Grammar School, where he edited the school magazine and took a leading part in school dramatic activities. After National Service in the Royal Army Pay Corps, he read geography at Selwyn, took a two-one, and joined the William Morris Institute of Automation Research, where he is now head of the Sport Department. He is married."

He examined his handiwork. It wasn't bad, if one looked at it in its context, which was accompanying a photograph of himself with a pipe and his profile shown up by skilful backlighting. He got the photograph out and held it above the paragraph he had typed.

Perhaps if the photograph were slightly broader? Or squarer? Or larger? Or perhaps the paragraph could be improved? The first two words were absolutely right. But after that, was it entirely worthy of the pipe? Did it carry through the rhythm established by the line of the jaw? He wound a fresh sheet of paper into the typewriter.

"Hugh Rowe," he wrote, "is a Londoner by birth, and comes of a family with the sea in its blood. His promise was already recognised by those in authority at the age of eleven. But he is more than a mere scholar. While still in his teens he was already working as a journalist and an actor, and before he was twenty he had responded to some romantic streak in his character by joining the army. His gallantry as a soldier was unquestioned. Now, as well as being one of the most promising writers of his generation, he is a leading figure in the exciting new field of automation research."

In a fury of perfectionism he tore the sheet out of the typewriter and started over again.

"Hugh Rowe," he wrote, "is one of the new polymaths. Journalist, writer, scientist, thinker, actor, soldier, wit, temporary postman—he has been all and more. . . ."

7

The soporific quiet which filled Goldwasser's laboratory in the Newspaper Department was disturbed only by the soft rustle of tired newsprint. Assistants bent over the component parts of the Department's united experiment, the demonstration that in theory a digital computer could be programmed to produce a perfectly satisfactory daily newspaper with all the variety and news sense of the old hand-made article. With silent, infinite tedium, they worked their way through stacks of newspaper cuttings, identifying the pattern of stories, and analysing the stories into standard variables and invariables. At other benches other assistants copied the variables and invariables down on to cards, and sorted the cards into filing cabinets, coded so that in theory a computer could pick its way from card to card in logical order and assemble a news item from them. Once Goldwasser and his colleagues had proved the theory, commercial interests would no doubt swiftly put it into practice. The stylisation of the modern newspaper would be complete. Its last residual connection with the raw, messy, offendable real world would have been broken.

Goldwasser picked up a completed file waiting for his attention. It was labelled "Paralysed Girl Determined to Dance Again." Inside it were forty-seven newspaper cuttings about paralysed girls who were determined to dance again. He put it to one side. He had picked it up, looked at the heading, and put it to one side every day for a week, waiting for a day when he felt strong.

He picked up the next file instead, labelled "Child Told Dress Unsuitable by Teacher." Inside there were ninety-five cuttings about children who had been told their dress was unsuitable by their teacher, an analysis of the cuttings into their elements, and a report from the researcher who had prepared the file. The report read:

"V. Satis. Basic plot entirely invariable. Variables confined to three. (1) Clothing objected to (high heels/petticoat/frilly knickers). (2) Whether child also smokes and/or uses lipstick. (3) Whether child alleged by parents to be humiliated by having offending clothing inspected before whole school.

"Frequency of publication: once every nine days."

Nobbs, Goldwasser's Principal Research Assistant, shambled over and threw some more files on to Goldwasser's desk. He wore a beard, to identify himself with the intelligentsia, affected a stooped, lounging gait to establish parity of esteem with the aristocracy, and called everyone except the Director and Deputy-Director "mate," to demonstrate solidarity with the proletariat. He had a powerful effect on Goldwasser, causing a helpless panic to seize him.

"Here you are, mate," said Nobbs, ramming the word "mate" into Goldwasser like a jack-knife. "I'm just doing the 'They Think Britain is Wonderful' file now. Seems all right. Variables are mainly who's doing the thinking—American tourists, Danish *au pair* girls, etc."

"Are you going to cross-index it with 'British Girls Are Best, Say Foreign Boys?'" said Goldwasser, "I mean, to avoid using them both on the same day?"

"It wouldn't matter, would it, mate?" said Nobbs. "We're trying for an upbeat tone overall, aren't we?"

"I suppose so," muttered Goldwasser, unable to bring himself to argue with anyone as horrible as Nobbs. "But cross-index it with 'Booming, Bustling Britain,' then. We can't have them *all* in on the same day."

"Your word is law, O master," said Nobbs. "Mate."

O God, prayed Goldwasser humanely, let Nobbs be painlessly destroyed.

"Have you checked 'Paralysed Girl Determined to Dance Again' yet?" asked Nobbs.

"Not yet," said Goldwasser.

"Well, don't blame me when we're a week behind schedule at the end of the month," said Nobbs. "That's all I ask, mate. And what about 'I Plan to Give Away My Baby, Says Mother-to-be'? We can't do anything more on that until we've got a policy decision from you."

"I'll look at that now," said Goldwasser. Nobbs slouched away. Goldwasser lifted his eyes from the pencil jar, where they had taken refuge from the sight of Nobbs, and watched Nobbs shamble back to his office, knocking over chairs and sweeping files off the corners of desks as he went. He turned to the "I Plan to Give Away My Baby, Says Mother-to-be" file.

"Difficulty here," said the researcher's report. "Frequency of once a month, but in fifty-three cuttings examined there are no variables at all. Even name of mother-to-be the same. May possibly involve fifty-three different, foetuses but no way of telling from cuttings. Can we use story with no variables?"

Goldwasser put it to one side. One had to wait for decisions as big as that to ambush one unexpectedly. He looked at his watch. He had the impression that he had been working continuously for an exceedingly long time. Perhaps he had earned a break; perhaps he could slip across to play with the loyal leader cards for five minutes.

Goldwasser sometimes took himself out of himself by pretending to be a computer, and going through one of the completed sets of cards observing the same logical rules and making the same random choices that a computer would to compose a story from them. The by-election set and the weather story set soon palled. So did "I Test New Car" and "Red Devils Fly In to Trouble Spot." But the set for composing a loyal leader on a royal occasion seemed to Goldwasser to have something of that teasing perfection which draws one back again and again to certain pictures.

He opened the filing cabinet and picked out the first card in the set. *Traditionally*, it read. Now there was a random choice between cards reading *coronations, engagements, funerals, weddings, coming of age, births, deaths*, or *the churching of women*. The day before he had picked *funerals*, and been directed on to a card reading with simple perfection *are occasions for mourning*. To-day he closed his eyes, drew *weddings*, and was signposted on to *are occasions for rejoicing*.

The wedding of X and Y followed in logical sequence, and brought him a choice between *is no exception* and *is a case in point*. Either way there followed *indeed*. Indeed, whichever occasion one had started off with, whether coronations, deaths, or births, Goldwasser saw with intense mathematical pleasure, one now reached this same elegant bottleneck. He paused on *indeed*, then drew in quick succession *it is a particularly happy occasion*, *rarely*, and *can there have been a more popular young couple*.

From the next selection Goldwasser drew *X has won himself/herself a special place in the nation's affections*, which forced him to go on to *and the British people have clearly taken Y to their hearts already*.

Goldwasser was surprised, and a little disturbed, to realise that the word "fitting" had still not come up. But he drew it with the next card—*it is especially fitting that*.

This gave him *the bride/bridegroom should be*, and an open choice between *of such a noble and illustrious line*, *a commoner in these democratic times*, *from a nation with which this country has long enjoyed a particularly close and cordial relationship*, and *from a nation with which this country's relations have not in the past been always happy*.

Feeling that he had done particularly well with "fitting" last time, Goldwasser now deliberately selected it again. *It is also fitting that*, read the card, to be quickly followed by *we should remember*, and *X and Y are not merely symbols—they are a lively young man and a very lovely young woman*.

Goldwasser shut his eyes to draw the next card. It turned out to read *in these days when*. He pondered whether to select *it is fashionable to scoff at the traditional morality of marriage and family life* or *it is no longer fashionable to scoff at the traditional morality of marriage and family life*. The latter had more of the form's

33

authentic baroque splendour, he decided. He drew another *it is fitting that*, but thinking three times round was once too many for anything, even for a superb and beautiful word like "fitting," he cheated and changed it for *it is meet that*, after which *we wish them well* followed as the night the day, and the entertainment was over.

What a piece of work had the school of Goldwasser wrought here! What a toccata and fugue! How remote it was from the harsh cares of life!

Goldwasser started all over again with the churching of women. He had got as far as a choice between *it is good to see the old traditions being kept up* and *it is good to see old usages brought more into line with our modern way of thinking*, when Nobbs came shambling out of his room, the word "mate" written all over his face.

"Now look here, mate," started Nobbs, "this Paralysed Girl Determined to Dance Again . . ."

But at this point, as it said on one of the cards in the "They Are Calling It the Street of Shame" story cabinet, *our investigator made an excuse and left.*

8

"But you said yourself," wheezed Dr. Jennifer Riddle, the Head of the Political Department, with furious indignation, "the Queen's visit was going to be an informal occasion with a minimum of fuss!"

Mrs. Plushkov, the Head of the International Affairs Department, watched her colleague with a slight smile of profound human sympathy. She was considering how One should deal with the situation in a way that combined both charity and practical effect. Certainly One should remain calm and graceful. One should try to feel sympathy for Riddle and her personality defects. Riddle was, after all, the greatest cross One had to bear, and One believed One could feel Oneself growing a little in grace even as One sympathised. In believing that, of course, One was making fun of Oneself: One's spiritual development could certainly be leavened with a little humour from time to time.

"What One said," she reminded Riddle kindly, "was that we should aim at an informal occasion from which we all emerged with dignity."

One bulked large in Mrs. Plushkov's life. She thought of little but One's obligations, One's position, One's self-respect. Ceaselessly and selflessly she considered what One should do, what One would like, how One would react. She wanted nothing for herself—had renounced all carnal desire in life but to do what One wanted and to make sure that everyone else did what One wanted as well.

Since One was a woman, One had an obligation to be unswervingly feminine. One had to be gracious. One had to speak with suitable sweetness. When something amusing was said, One had a polite duty to smile a modest, gracious smile, and when the joke was over One had to fold One's smile up and put it tidily away so that One could find it readily for use on another occasion. It was scarcely surprising that not only Mrs. Plushkov but everybody else in the Institute was in awe of One. It was even less surprising that One had been entrusted with the arrangements for the Queen's visit. If One had a local mono-poly of savoir-faire, as One apparently did, then One had a certain duty on these occasions.

Riddle, who had been sitting perched on the edge of Mrs. Plushkov's desk with one laddered knee only a few inches away from Mrs. Plushkov's face, got off, and began to stride up and down the laboratory with her hands behind her back. One watched her, One's spiritual development furthered by every aspect of the scene. There were three large grease-spots on the lapel of Riddle's jacket, and an unidentifiable hardened green-ish stain down the back of her skirt. Her spectacles were so dirty as to be almost opaque, and her ferociously permed hair appeared to be held in place by several paper-clips and a rub-ber sealing band from the inside of a tobacco tin. A cigarette—or, as Riddle always called it, a fag—hung permanently from the corner of her mouth, making her perpetually choke and cough. The smoke rising from it made her eyes water, and the ash and red-hot fragments falling from it scattered liberally over the vases of flowers, silver paper-knives, petit-point computer covers, and other civilising touches with which One had brightened One's laboratory.

"I mean," said Riddle, gasping in air through her teeth, "you know my view. I regard the whole undertaking as a load of com-plete bloody balls from beginning to end."

One smiled. Perhaps, Mrs. Plushkov was thinking, Riddle was completely unlobbyable. Perhaps even attempting to lobby her was nothing but spiritual selfishness—merely making use of her as a rack on which to grow in grace. Mrs. Plushkov attached a great deal of importance to lobbying. She had had all the Heads of Departments to tea in her laboratory one by one, sounding them out, soliciting their support for this against that, arranging caucuses to stop rival caucuses. This, as One knew from a wide reading of the appropriate literature, was the way these things were done on the High Table of an academic institution.

"Another cup of tea," she suggested, taking the little kettle off the spirit lamp on her desk and recharging the silver teapot. Riddle grasped the delicate porcelain cup in her fist and held it out, breathing hard, and bringing two or three large flakes of ash down to float in the cream jug.

"That's another thing," she gasped. "Tea. The Committee voted to offer the Queen a cup of tea. I know—I was there. Now I hear we're going to provide a whole running buffet."

Mrs. Plushkov sighed almost imperceptibly. When she had been asked to make the arrangements for the Queen's visit, she had been supplied with an Organising Committee to assist her, to which all the Heads of Departments were appointed. The existence of the Committee had of course greatly increased her work. One knew about committees; One could not allow matters to go into the public glare of open committee until they had been thoroughly settled behind the scenes. If the Committee were allowed to become a forum of debate instead of a ceremonial organ for formalising decisions already taken, the most ungraceful scenes could occur. People might lose their tempers, haggle, shout, be driven into extreme positions, bring things up which never should be brought up in public, and generally make an unappetising spectacle of themselves. So she had undertaken her labour of patient lobbying.

Even so, One could not help regretting that it had been necessary to have a Committee at all. Eventually resolutions had to be recorded, and however carefully framed they were so as not to commit One to anything unfortunate, they were always rich material for misunderstanding for those who wished to misunderstand them. Riddle and others had a habit of interpreting the Committee's resolutions with an extraordinarily primitive literalism. Riddle in particular seemed to believe that when the Committee had declared it was in favour

37

of an informal occasion without excessive protocol or hand-shaking, it meant that the staff would stand around with their hands in their pockets, and greet the Queen with a curt nod! And when the Committee had resolved to give the Queen tea, it seemed that some people had thought it meant just that—handing her a plastic Tea Room cup of cooling Tea Room tea!

"My dear Riddle," said Mrs. Plushkov with unending patience, "when the Committee mentioned informality One can be perfectly certain that it did not mean downright rudeness."

"Look, old cock, no one's suggested being rude ..."

"Similarly, my dear Riddle, when it resolved to offer her tea I think One can be fairly sure it did not exclude the possibility that she would like a biscuit or a slice of cake to go with it."

"Or a slice of smoked salmon? Or a caviare sandwich?"

"Possibly. The exact range of the refreshments has not yet been decided on."

"For all you know, it might include roast peacock and stuffed boar's head?"

"I don't think the Catering Sub-Committee are likely to want to include anything as heavy as that."

"Oh, there's a *Catering* Sub-Committee now, is there? As well as the Refreshments Committee? Look, old cock, this thing's getting out of hand."

For a moment Mrs. Plushkov's smile disappeared. Riddle had touched on a sensitive spot. The annoying thing was that the proliferation of committees was something One had started Oneself. To avoid unseemly outbursts from Riddle in the Organising Committee, One had referred all questions which might have provoked them—which was to say, all questions—to special sub-committees which did not include Riddle. Of course, the thing had to be done discreetly, without arousing the suspicions of Riddle's potential allies—Goldwasser, Macintosh, Rowe, and others—so that as a smoke-screen a number of extra sub-committees had to be set up which included Riddle. The sting was taken out of these by requiring them to report back to a Joint Advisory Council, on which Riddle was not represented.

By a deft manœuvre Riddle got herself appointed to a Procedure Committee to co-ordinate the work of all those sub-committees on which she did not sit. Mrs. Plushkov replied by setting up a Co-ordinating Committee, without Riddle, to co-ordinate the work of the Joint Advisory Council and the Procedure Committee, which then set up Working Parties to study the implementation of the proposals put forward by the various sub-committees.

One had felt at first that this complexity was of some value in itself, since it increased the probability that One was the only person who could understand and therefore control it. But at a certain point a curious thing had happened. The organism had gone critical. When the total number of committees, sub-committees, and working parties had reached twenty-three, cell division began to occur spontaneously. One day there were twenty-three organisational units, for all of which One could account, and the next day there were twenty-four. Mrs. Plushkov found the minutes of a body called the Central Liaison Committee being circulated—a committee of which One had never heard, and which included neither Riddle nor One. And the next day there were twenty-six committees! The monster had come alive!

"Be that as it may," said Mrs. Plushkov, allowing herself to imply a suspicion of reproachfulness against Riddle by spooning some of the ash out of the cream jug, "One must leave catering matters to the Catering Sub-Committee. What One really ought to discuss is the question—which I believe is coming up in your Procedure Committee tomorrow—of the Protocol Committee's report on the press enclosure."

"The *what*?" croaked Riddle.

Mrs. Plushkov smiled with charity.

"The enclosure for the journalists reporting the visit," she said.

"*What* journalists reporting the visit?"

"A number of reporters and photographers will be given passes by the Palace press authorities. It's done on a rota system—it's quite out of our hands."

"Then what's this enclosure business?"

"I believe what the Protocol Committee had in mind was that certain precautions were necessary if the press were going to have access to alcohol."

"Just a moment, old lad. What's this about alcohol?"

"The Protocol Committee believes—and One feels rightly—that we should offer the press drinks. Apparently it's customary on these occasions."

"Why can't they have tea like everyone else?"

"Apparently the press doesn't drink tea. Anyway, it's proposed that the press should be separated from the royal party by either red plush ropes with brass mountings, or a dense screen of indoor vegetation. One doesn't want some drunken reporter leaning over the barrier and trying to touch the Queen. Then again, One can scarcely ignore the possibility that one of them will start throwing things. They will be much less tempted to throw things, the Protocol Committee believes, if they cannot see what to throw them at."

Riddle choked with rage and smoke.

"I thought this was supposed to be an informal visit," she gasped.

"One can surely take it pretty much for granted that One should not allow informality to be taken to the point where the Queen would find herself greeted by a fusillade of crab sandwiches and empty liquor bottles."

Riddle slapped down her cup, and drew in a supply of air with which to shout, "I shall fight this every inch of the way," before marching out of the room. But the cold air tickled her smoke-raw throat, and she suffered a prolonged fit of coughing, by the end of which the moment for rhetoric seemed to have passed.

Nevertheless, she did fight it every inch of the way, and in most of the committees that had anything to do with the matter she eventually won. It was, so she, Goldwasser, Macintosh and Rowe agreed, a famous victory for the forces of reason.

All the same, both the red plush ropes and the dense screen

of indoor vegetation were ordered from the contractors. It was Miss Fram, Nunn's secretary, who was actually responsible for putting the recommendations of the various committees into effect, and she didn't take too much notice of what committees said. Everyone knew that committees were not very good at this sort of thing. And it seemed to Miss Fram that though the visit ought to be an informal one, informality should not be taken to the point where the Queen would find herself greeted by a fusillade of crab sandwiches and empty liquor bottles.

9

"Yes," said Rowe thoughtfully, "yes." He might not be as intelligent as Macintosh, he reflected, and in conversation with Macintosh he might not say very much, but at least what he did say was said only after hard and sincere thought. Looking at Macintosh across their empty coffee-cups in the Tea Room at the Institute, he wondered whether he had said enough to make Macintosh fully aware of the fierce intensity of his thought. "Yes," he said again, as if the words being dragged from him were the sole survivors of an exhausting civil war among themselves, "yes."

"I like to philosophise a little," said Macintosh. "As you know, I like to reflect a little on the terrifying grandeur of our work, the sadness and the hugeness of it all."

"Yes," said Rowe.

"Take your department, Rowe. Now, you're producing a programme which will permit all the bingo games in the country to be run simultaneously from one central computer. Well, that's obvious. It had to come. There's nothing very revolutionary about putting such a purely mechanical process of randomising and correlating out to a computer."

"No, no."

"Then you'll start producing a programme for automating the football results. Again, it had to come. Professional football is becoming increasingly uneconomic, but the pools industry has to carry on somehow. It doesn't take even the stupidest wee businessman long to see that paying twenty-two men to do nothing but make a random choice between win, lose, and draw is economic madness. Once you've done football it won't take people long to see that you can replace all the racecourses in the country with one quite simple and inexpensive computer. And of course cricket. When takings at the gate have fallen low enough to cure any tendency to sentiment, people will notice that a computer is a far more suitable tool than a cricket team for producing a complex score sheet from the variables of ground moisture, light, surface wear on ball, fallibility of wicket-keeper, and so on. In fact all the complex mass of statistics produced by the sports industry can without exception be produced not only more economically by computer, but also with more significant patterns and more amazing freaks. I take it that the main object of organised sports and games is to produce a profusion of statistics?"

"Oh, yes," said Rowe. "So far as I know."

"No one has ever suggested any other reason, have they?"

"I don't think so."

"No, of course not. But one needs to get these fundamental considerations straight before one builds on them. Anyway, if that is so, I think we can assume that a computer is a more efficient statistics-producing machine than any possible combination of horses, dogs, or muscular young men. But that's not the end of it. For what have we shown? That any human activity which consists of repetition, or of manipulating variables identifiable in advance according to predetermined rules, or of manipulating a known range of variables at random, can in theory at any rate be performed by a computer."

"Yes," said Rowe. "That's really the basic, er, the basic. . ."

". . . principle on which our work is founded. So it is. So we automate the bingo industry. But now consider the activity of the person who plays bingo. Isn't his activity—covering the numbers on a board as they are called and signalling when a certain pattern is completed—precisely analogous? Couldn't *his* work be done for him by a computer fed with a very simple programme indeed?"

"Yes," said Rowe. "Yes, it could."

"And will be. No one is going to spend hours in a bingo hall if he can simply pay over his money and have a computer play for him instead. Filling up a football coupon is another job

43

which a computer could easily be programmed to do. You could set it to fill the coupon at random, or to make a selection based on any system you liked, or to select its own system, or to choose between a random choice and a system of its own choosing. Once again we have a range of variables which can be identified in advance and manipulated according to predetermined rules. It's programmable. Having a man to perform it is a waste of time."

"Y-e-e-e-es," said Rowe. "Y-e-e-e-es."

"And when you come to think about it, you could programme a computer to appreciate the cricket results for you— or even to appreciate the actual automated game as the playing computer played it. It would be instructed to register applause at amazing freaks—at, say, the announcement of a slip catch off a fast bowler in poor light. It would register annoyance when the side it was instructed to identify with suffered a reverse— annoyance mixed with reluctant admiration if it was the result of the other side's skill. It would be programmed to register boredom when nothing unusual happened for some time— without any boredom being inflicted on any actual human being."

"But the point of watching cricket, surely," said Rowe, "is actually to see and appreciate the skill of the players."

"Then why are so many people content to listen to it being described on the wireless? In either case the activity of the spectator or the listener is the same—to register a selection from a range of reactions in correlation to the permutations of variables he is offered. So far as I can see, it's a finite activity, which means it's a programmable one. The spectator is eminently replaceable."

"But," said Rowe, "the spectator *enjoys* watching."

"He may, I suppose, but that's rather beside the point. The hydraulic press operator who is replaced by a computer when his factory is automated may enjoy operating a hydraulic press. But that doesn't save him from being replaced. A human being, my dear Rowe, is far too complex and expensive an instrument

44

to be wasted on simple finite tasks like operating presses, filling up football pools, and watching cricket. The whole world of sport, I believe, will gradually become an entirely enclosed one, unvisited by any human being except the maintenance engineers. Computers will play. Computers will watch. Computers will comment. Computers will store results, and pit their memories against other computers in sports quiz programmes on the television organised by computers and watched by computers."

"Y-e-e-e-s," said Rowe.

"Still, that's all your department. I expect you have all this covered already."

"Well, you know . . ."

"There's lots to do, Rowe. I'm hog-tied by my Samaritan programme, as you know, but if I had the time to move into my new wing I'd like to take over some of the work Riddle and Plushkov are doing in the Political and International Affairs departments. If diplomacy and party politics were conducted by computers, Rowe, there'd be much less danger of them being deflected from sound old preconceived ideas by intransigent realities. That's how I should like to see our affairs conducted, because that's the way I'm made myself. I have a strange drive to monomania, Rowe, a subconscious desire to be automatable."

"I see."

"Then again, I'd rather like to open a Rituals Department. If only I had the time! We could do everything from the Trooping the Colour and the Honours Lists, down to the official opening of the new wing. Oh, the money and time and manpower we could save! And the unspeakable load of boredom we could lift from people's shoulders! But then, if only I had the time to go into the new wing, there's no end to the things I could start programming. One of my pet projects is a programme for eliminating middlemen from the distributive trades by calculating their usual profit for them without the need to have them involved. And have I told you about my idea of programming a computer to write pornographic novels? They're all permutations of a very small range of finite variables—you could do it on quite a

45

simple computer. Or sex manuals—even fewer basic possibilities, and an apparently insatiable market for permutations of them. Still, I think I prefer pornography myself. It has a certain stark, logical grandeur which I enjoy—among other things, of course."

"Yes," said Rowe. His mind, when Macintosh stopped speaking, went on to traverse great terrains of still unthought thoughts. It was tumultuous, raging country. If he could just struggle to a vantage point and look down on it quietly for a moment he could map it out in words. Far wilder regions than even Macintosh had explored, their fantastic contours almost clear to the inward eye. If he could just . . . just . . .

"Yes," he said. "Yes."

10

Sir Prestwick Wining was not good on the telephone. It was an instrument which had made a fool of better men than him. How could one possibly tell if the voice at the other end was who it said it was, or meant what it said it meant, or was what it seemed, or seemed what it was?

"Nunn? Hallo, Nunn?" he demanded anxiously. He was anxious lest Nunn was absent, or dead, and he had only been put through to him as some sort of practical joke.

"Nunn? Are you there, Nunn?" he said fiercely. The panic rose within him. Was Nunn at the other end of the line or was he not? Perhaps he *was* dead. He could imagine bevy upon bevy of telephone girls listening in at every junction of the line and giggling helplessly because they had made him shout at Nunn when Nunn was dead, lying in state on top of his desk.

"Nunn!" he cried unhappily. "Nunn!"

" 'Morning, Sir Prestwick," said Nunn, who had been obliged to finish dealing with a rather tricky leg-spinner from the hat-stand end.

"Is that you, Nunn?"

"Speaking, Sir Prestwick."

"Ah. I was trying to get you, Nunn. Now, Nunn . . . Hallo? Nunn? Nunn? Nunn, are you there or aren't you?"

Nunn was watching the leg-spinner, which he had hooked away through the mid-carpet, and which had now just evaded square leg by the waste-paper basket and gone for four, to warmly appreciative applause, by the radiator.

"Sorry, Sir Prestwick. Rather a lot going on at this end. Fire away."

"I see. Now, Nunn . . ."

"Did you see the show-jumping your competitors were televising last night?"

"No. Now, Nunn . . ."

"Some very pretty jumping. Sorry, I interrupted you."

"Yes, well . . ."

"Mind was wandering. Sign of old age."

"Ah. Now a most . . ."

"Unforgivable rudeness. I hate being interrupted myself."

"Nunn, a most serious contingency has arisen."

"Aha."

"Your plans for the new wing. I'm afraid Rothermere won't wear them."

"Oh?"

"Rothermere's clear understanding—and I have a letter before me from your Miss Fram to this effect—was that the wing would be used, and I quote, 'to extend the work of the Ethics Department in investigating to what extent computers can be programmed to follow codes of ethical behaviour.'"

"That's right."

"Well, we offered our support for this work, Nunn, in the belief that it was helping to combat teenage deliquency and immorality. That is what the word 'ethics' suggests to us."

"That's what it suggests to me too, Sir Prestwick."

"Well. Rothermere fails to understand—and I fail to understand—how this could justify using the wing to get computers writing pornographic novels and sex manuals."

"Pornographic novels and sex manuals?"

"Exactly."

"We're going to have computers writing them, are we?"

"So I'm told."

"In the new wing?"

"Apparently. Rothermere heard about it from some girl he met at a party."

"Are you sure she knew what was going on here?"

"Apparently she said she'd had it from a man who said it was all over the Institute."

"I see. Well, I'll look into it."

"I mean, I shouldn't like you to think we were trying to influence the work being done in the new wing just because we've put up the money."

"Of course not."

"Nothing further from our minds. Rothermere would never dream of doing anything like that."

"Of course he wouldn't."

"It's just that we have to be careful what the Company's name is associated with."

"Exactly. Exactly. Of course, I never interfere in the running of the departments, as I'm sure you'll understand."

"Oh, of course."

"But I'll certainly put my foot down on any nonsense about pornographic novels and sex manuals."

"Well, I told Rothermere we could rely on you."

"Only too pleased to help."

"There's nothing personal in this, Nunn."

"Of course not."

"But I've had Rothermere on to me all morning about it. I hope I didn't sound sharp?"

"You'd have been fully justified. Fully justified."

"I mean, Rothermere's rather a stickler for this sort of thing. And frankly, after a whole morning of it the old tummy starts to play up a bit."

"Leave it to me. I'll have a word with Macintosh right away."

"I suppose Macintosh does have his heart in the new wing?"

"Oh, a hundred per cent."

"Really? I couldn't help getting the impression he was a bit luke-warm when I met him."

"No, no, keen as mustard."

"I mean, he kept saying he didn't want the wing and he wouldn't have anything to do with it."

"Oh, that's just his way of expressing himself. Queer fellows, these scientific johnnies."

"I suppose they are."

"Never cease to astonish me."

"No."

"Right you are, then."

"So you'll get on to Macintosh?"

"I'll get on to Macintosh."

"All right, then."

"Thanks for letting me know."

"No, thank you."

"I'll get on to Macintosh right away."

"You'll get on to him, will you?"

"Right away."

"There we are then."

"I think that covers everything."

"I think so."

"Well, then . . ."

"Well, if you'll get on to Macintosh."

"Yes, I'll get on to Macintosh."

"I think that's it, then."

"I think it should be."

"If there's anything else we can always ring one another again."

"Of course we can."

"Well, then, my compliments to your good lady."

11

"Hugh Rowe," wrote Hugh Rowe, "has given us a brilliant first novel. Warm, witty, wise—*R* is compulsively readable from first page to last. I have no hesitation at all in choosing it as my Book of the Year."

Goldwasser came into the laboratory.

"I saw you at it again out of my window. Couldn't resist coming down for a closer look."

"Oh?" said Rowe.

"R," he wrote, "*opens a new and exciting era in the development of the novel as an art form.*"

"Your novel, is it?" asked Goldwasser.

"Yes," said Rowe. He wrote: "*A hit! A hit! A palpable hit!*"

"What sort of novel is it?" asked Goldwasser.

"*Dynamic, devastating,*" wrote Rowe. He said: "Oh, you know, the usual sort of thing."

"Oh?"

"*I humbly urge everyone,*" wrote Rowe, "*to read this truly remarkable document at the earliest possible opportunity.*"

"May I read it?" asked Goldwasser.

"Read it? Oh, well, it's not really ready for . . . I mean, when it's finished, of course . . ."

But Goldwasser was already looking over Rowe's shoulder.

"I see," he said after a moment. "God, I'm terribly sorry, Rowe! I mean, I didn't realise . . . It was unforgivable of me."

"The point is," said Rowe, "I've decided to write the reviews first . . ."

"First? You mean the novel's not even written?"

"No. You see, Goldwasser, I thought I'd do the reviews first, and then as it were reconstruct the novel from them."

"I see."

"I mean, writers work in different ways."

"Yes."

"You don't think it's unreasonable to go about it this way round?"

"Oh, no."

"I mean, I sometimes wonder a bit myself."

"You do?"

"Oh, yes. It's a horribly lonely business, writing. One sometimes wonders if one hasn't somehow—well—left the rails."

Goldwasser thought for a bit.

"Rowe," he said. "Do you have a plot for this novel? Or any characters?"

Rowe gazed silently at his typewriter. Terrible, tormenting, and true, he thought. Wicked relevance and devastating accuracy. Goes to the heart of the problem.

"I'm feeling my way towards them," he said.

"I see. Do you have any other—what shall I say?—point of departure fixed?"

"Well," said Rowe. He knew what he wanted to write, but he couldn't say it. Or write it, really. He couldn't say it or write it because the visions he wished to describe were as warm and fugitive as dreams. The more you try to describe a dream the further it eludes your grasp, retreating before the advance of the words, growing cooler and cooler and paler and paler, until, when you have recorded it all, there is nothing of what it was really like left in your memory. Rowe wanted to write about scenes that came to him suddenly when his brain was warm, and seemed for an instant to contain the whole sweetness of life. There was a scene where a sharp March wind drove flickering pale sunshine across an industrial estuary. There was a scene where tired, half-innocent eyes saw the first grey light of a summer's day spread over poplars and copper beeches in full leaf, and stone balustrades, and lawns white with dew. There was a scene where he walked through the fog on a November evening, and breathed out more fog into the yellow haze beneath a street lamp, and heard a motor-cycle engine ticking over, going "dyna-dyna-dyna-dyna." But how to begin to write them down so that even the smallest residue of their preciousness remained he had no idea.

"No?" said Goldwasser.

"Not in concrete terms."

"You don't want to put forward some thesis? You don't want to illustrate how power corrupts, or desire destroys? You don't want to show up the petty-mindedness of life at provincial universities, or the ruthlessness of college politics at Oxford and Cambridge?"

"I don't think so, on the whole."

"Well, let's start with some characters and a plot, then. First we want a hero. Let's say his name is Eye. Now, I take it that Eye has an affair with someone."

"Yew?"

"A bit unsubtle. How about Mi—short for Wilhelmina? Now we're getting somewhere. Mi is married, of course, to a dull, middle-aged publisher called Howard. For years their marriage has been a sham. Then Eye, a passionate young writer rebelling against the stuffed-shirt conventions that surround him, urges Mi to come away with him and start a new, genuine life together."

"That's good, Goldwasser!"

"We've scarcely started yet. Now, Howard has a mistress, Lisbeth. Lisbeth and Mi meet and feel a strange attraction to one another. Filled with terrible doubts that she is really a Lesbian, Mi tries to break off the affair with Eye, and hurls herself into a deliberately sordid and degrading affair with Leo, Lisbeth's drunken playboy half-brother. In a desperate attempt to console himself for the loss of Mi, Eye sleeps with Lisbeth, but Lisbeth admits that she has once had an incestuous relationship with Leo, and Eye, overcome by a profound spiritual disgust with life, suddenly becomes a homosexual, and allows himself to be seduced by Howard."

"Goldwasser, this is the real stuff!"

"I haven't finished yet. What Eye doesn't know, of course, is that Howard is only doing it to revenge himself on Leo for Leo's affair with Mi."

"I don't think I quite get that."

"Well, Howard and Leo have of course been having a homosexual relationship for years. It was Leo's only real human relationship, and when he hears that Howard has deceived him with Eye, he goes off on a prolonged orgy which kills him. When Lisbeth hears about Leo's death she commits suicide. Eye feels somehow responsible for Lisbeth's death and goes insane. With no one left to turn to, Howard and Mi resume their life together, to spend the rest of their lives torturing one another with blame and remorse."

"That really is a *plot*, Goldwasser!"

"It's the best I can do off the cuff, anyway."

"I think it's absolutely staggering."

"With a bit of work on it you could make it much more complex."

Rowe thought about it for some minutes. "Goldwasser, you don't think there are too *many* sexual relationships in it?"

"How could there be? That's what novels are about."

"I suppose they are."

"Well, they haven't thought of anything else, have they?"

"I suppose they haven't. You know, I hadn't looked at it like that."

"I can't imagine what you were thinking of writing a novel about if not sexual relationships."

"Well, I had part of an idea. It's difficult to explain, but it was about a man walking along a street. In a fog."

"And what happens?"

"He breathes out."

"He breathes out?"

"And then he hears a motor-bike."

"Then what happens?"

"I don't know. I hadn't really finished working it out, of course."

Goldwasser rubbed his cheek.

"You could bring it in," he said. "I suppose."

"Perhaps Eye could walk down the street in the fog on his way from Mi to Lisbeth?"

"Or on his way from Lisbeth to Howard."

"I suppose so."

"You could put it in almost anywhere."

"Y-e-e-e-s."

"Well, I'll leave you to it."

After Goldwasser had gone, Rowe wound a fresh sheet of paper into the typewriter. He had known that the requirements of the novel form would catch up on him sooner or later, but he had imagined that he might be able to stave them off at least until he had written the extended critical appreciation for *Encounter*.

"Hugh Rowe," he found his fingers typing gloomily, "has not written the totally original masterpiece that some commentators expected from him. But *A Knot of Worms* is a competent, work-manlike novel, whose strength lies in the stark realism of its plot, which boldly faces up to life as it is lived in the modern novel. . . ."

12

"Ah! Afternoon, Macintosh," said Nunn. "Nice of you to look in. Take a pew. That's right, chuck those rugger boots off on to the floor. Smoke? No? Sensible man, sensible man."

Nunn's hand imperceptibly noted in his Compleat Angler's Diary "Mac. v. defensive." Of course, he was going to put him at his ease before he interrogated him. Standard procedure.

"Fish?" he asked pleasantly.

"What?" said Macintosh.

"Fish?"

"Er, not now, thanks."

"Not now?"

"I've just had lunch."

"Ah."

Nunn's hand moved over the diary again. "Mac. v. evasive," he noted.

"I was only going to say," he said, "that it was a good day for it."

"A good day for fish?"

"Yes—it's a wet day."

"Oh. I thought Friday was the great day for fish?"

"A fine day? Oh, no—a wet day."

"I see."

Brilliant these scientist laddies may be, thought Nunn, but ordinary human communication with them was well-nigh impossible.

"Now look, Macintosh," said Nunn. "Let me speak to you quite frankly. As you know, I never interfere in the running of the departments. Couldn't if I wanted to. I'm not a computer man myself, of course, and I don't know the first thing about the work."

"No."

"And of course the Director and I have absolutely full confidence in you. Full confidence."

"Good."

"But the point is this, Macintosh—and I'll be absolutely frank about it. I was having a word with Sir Prestwick Wining this morning. Do you know him?"

"I've met him."

"Of course you have. Anyway, he was saying what a tremendous respect Rothermere Vulgurian had for the Institute's academic freedom."

"Oh?"

"Yes. Apparently he's very anxious that the new wing should be independent in every way. He doesn't want us to feel that because he's putting up the money he has any influence over the work that's being done in it at all."

"I'm pleased to hear it."

"I should think that you as the Head of the department must find that particularly satisfying. Well, of course, that rather puts the ball in our court. The more freedom Vulgurian gives us, the more careful we must be not to abuse it. I'm sure you see that."

"Yes."

"Of course, these things wouldn't matter quite so much in the normal course of events. But with the Queen coming down for the opening the Institute's going to be rather in the glare of publicity. So academic freedom apart, we must take jolly good care we don't drop our friends at Amalgamated Television in the soup in any way. I take it I'm making myself clear?"

"Clear as mud."

"Jolly good. A word to the wise, eh? I knew you'd take the point."

"Oh?"

"I mean, people talk a lot of nonsense about scientists being difficult people to get through to. But I say, if a chap's a decent chap, he's a decent chap be he a scientist or a nigger minstrel."

"I see."

"Of course you do. I mean, I wouldn't have mentioned it at

57

all, only you know how careful these television companies have to be about public opinion. So when I heard what you were up to over there in the new wing ..."

"Up to?"

"I mean, I know it's all done from purely scientific interest."

"I'm not up to anything in the new wing."

"No, well, strictly speaking ..."

"That's the whole point."

"Well, yes, I see that. You mean, you never were up to anything anyway?"

"I keep telling you—I'm not doing anything at all in the new wing."

"Well, I tried to explain that to Sir Prestwick."

"Good."

"I mean, I told him right away. 'Look,' I said, 'I don't know where you've got this from, but let me assure you here and now that Macintosh is not up to anything at all in that new wing.' "

"I mean ..."

" 'I know Macintosh pretty well,' I said, 'and I can tell you he's just not that sort of chap.' "

"I mean, it's not as if I haven't explained ..."

"Well, that's exactly what I told Sir Prestwick. 'It's a lot of rubbish,' I told him, 'and you can jolly well go back to whoever you got it from and tell him I said so.'"

"Yes ..."

"I mean, Sir Prestwick's a nice chap and all that, but I sometimes feel he's not terribly sound. Too much of a yes-man. Always agrees with both sides. Well, it can't be done."

"No."

"There we are, then. I knew Sir Prestwick had got it back-to-front all along. Nice of you to drop in and help clear it up."

As Macintosh got up to go, Nunn noted in his diary: "Mac. v. co-operative."

"Just one thing," he said. "Strictly off the record, of course, but if you ever *did* get your jolly old machines turning out dirty books, I'd be rather interested to have a look at them."

13

If Goldwasser was remembered for nothing else, Macintosh once told Rowe, he would be remembered for his invention of UHL.

UHL was Unit Headline Language, and it consisted of a comprehensive lexicon of all the multi-purpose monosyllables used by headline-writers. Goldwasser's insight had been to see that if the grammar of "ban," "dash," "fear," and the rest was ambiguous they could be used in almost any order to make a sentence, and that if they could be used in almost any order to make a sentence they could be easily randomised. Here then was one easy way in which a computer could find material for an automated newspaper—put together a headline in basic UHL first and then fit the story to it.

UHL, Goldwasser quickly realised, was an ideal answer to the problem of making a story run from day to day in an automated paper. Say, for example, that the randomiser turned up

STRIKE THREAT

By adding one unit at random to the formula each day the story could go:

STRIKE THREAT BID
STRIKE THREAT PROBE
STRIKE THREAT PLEA

And so on. Or the units could be added cumulatively:

STRIKE THREAT PLEA
STRIKE THREAT PLEA PROBE
STRIKE THREAT PLEA PROBE MOVE
STRIKE THREAT PLEA PROBE MOVE SHOCK
STRIKE THREAT PLEA PROBE MOVE SHOCK HOPE
STRIKE THREAT PLEA PROBE MOVE SHOCK HOPE STORM

Or the units could be used entirely at random:

LEAK ROW LOOMS

TEST ROW LEAK

LEAK HOPE DASH BID

TEST DEAL RACE

HATE PLEA MOVE

RACE HATE PLEA MOVE DEAL

Such headlines, moreover, gave a newspaper a valuable air of dealing with serious news, and helped to dilute its obsession with the frilly-knickeredness of the world, without alarming or upsetting the customers. Goldwasser had had a survey conducted, in fact, in which 457 people were shown the headlines

ROW HOPE MOVE FLOP

LEAK DASH SHOCK

HATE BAN BID PROBE

Asked if they thought they understood the headlines, 86.4 per cent said yes, but of these 97.3 per cent were unable to offer any explanation of what it was they had understood. With UHL, in other words, a computer could turn out a paper whose language was both soothingly familiar and yet calmingly incomprehensible.

Goldwasser sometimes looked back to the time when he had invented UHL as a lost golden age. That was before Nobbs had risen to the heights of Principal Research Assistant, and with it his beardedness and his belief in the universal matehood of man. In those days Goldwasser was newly appointed Head of his department. He had hurried eagerly to work each day in whatever clothes first came to hand in his haste. He had thought nothing of founding a new inter-language before lunch, arguing with Macintosh through the midday break, devising four news categories in the afternoon, then taking Macintosh and his new wife out to dinner, going on to a film, and finishing up playing chess with Macintosh into the small hours. In those days he had been fairly confident that he was cleverer than Macintosh. He had even been fairly confident that Macintosh had thought he was cleverer than Macintosh. In those days Macintosh had been his Principal Research Assistant.

It was difficult not to believe the world was deteriorating when one considered the replacement of Macintosh by Nobbs. Goldwasser sometimes made a great effort to see the world remaining—as he believed it did—much as it always was, and to see Nobbs as a potential Macintosh to a potential incoming Goldwasser. It was not easy. Now that Macintosh had gone on to become Head of the Ethics Department, Goldwasser no longer invented his way through a world of clear, cerebral TEST PLEA DASH SHOCK absolutes. Now his work seemed ever more full of things like the crash survey.

The crash survey showed that people were not interested in reading about road crashes unless there were at least ten dead. A road crash with ten dead, the majority felt, was slightly less interesting than a rail crash with one dead, unless it had piquant details—the ten dead turning out to be five still virginal honeymoon couples, for example, or pedestrians mown down by the local J.P. on his way home from a hunt ball. A rail crash was always entertaining, with or without children's toys still lying pathetically among the wreckage. Even a rail crash on the Continent made the grade provided there were at least five dead. If it was in the United States the minimum number of dead rose to twenty; in South America 100; in Africa 200; in China 500.

But people really preferred an air crash. Here, curiously enough, people showed much less racial discrimination. If the crash was outside Britain, 50 dead Pakistanis or 50 dead Filipinos were as entertaining as 50 dead Americans. What people enjoyed most was about 70 dead, with some 20 survivors including children rescued after at least one night in open boats. They liked it to be backed up with a story about a middle-aged housewife who had been booked to fly aboard the plane but who had changed her mind at the last moment.

Goldwasser was depressed for a month over the crash survey. But he could not see any way of producing a satisfactory automated newspaper without finding these things out. Now he was depressed all over again as he formulated the questions to be asked in the murder survey.

His draft ran:

1. Do you prefer to read about a murder in which the victim is (*a*) a small girl (*b*) an old lady (*c*) an illegitimately pregnant young woman (*d*) a prostitute (*e*) a Sunday school teacher?

2. Do you prefer the alleged murderer to be (*a*) a Teddy boy (*b*) a respectable middle-aged man (*c*) an obvious psychopath (*d*) the victim's spouse or lover (*e*) a mental defective?

3. Do you prefer a female corpse to be naked, or to be clad in underclothes?

4. Do you prefer any sexual assault involved to have taken place before or after death?

5. Do you prefer the victim to have been (*a*) shot (*b*) strangled (*c*) stabbed (*d*) beaten to death (*e*) kicked to death (*f*) left to die of exposure?

6. Do you prefer the murder to have taken place in a milieu which seems (*a*) exotic (*b*) sordid (*c*) much like your own and the people next door's?

7. If (*c*) do you prefer the case to reveal that beneath the surface life was (*a*) as apparently respectable as on the surface (*b*) a hidden cesspit of vice and degradation?

Nobbs enjoyed the survey. " 'Do you prefer a female corpse to be naked, or to be clad in underclothes?' " he repeated to Goldwasser. "That's what I call a good question, mate. That's what I call a good question."

Goldwasser, his heart heavy, sought refuge from Nobbs and his own questions in several new volumes of IQ tests which a friend in America had sent him. They were beautiful questions, with beautiful answers, and for a few hours they made the world's more horrible contents seem infinitely remote and insignificant. And the results gave his graph for the quarter a slight and credible upward gradient.

14

The Security Committee, which was Nunn, was much occupied with the problem of Riddle, the Head of the Political Department. The Committee, or rather Miss Fram, took up copies of the minutes of all the other committees and filed them in a filing cabinet labelled, for security reasons, Sporting Records. When Nunn could spare the time from squash and rugby he browsed through them, looking for any signs of security weakness. What he saw confirmed his instinctive distrust of four of the Heads of Departments—Macintosh, Goldwasser, Rowe, and Riddle. It was difficult to put one's finger on it exactly, but to the trained eye of an old security hand there was something dissident about those four, some residual permanent narkedness, something irreducibly antipathetic to the general idea of champagne, picture hats, official handshakes, and curtsies in shapeless silk dresses. Nunn had met their type before. Sportingly tolerant though one was, one could not but be put on one's guard by the lack of enthusiasm with which such people scrummed down on the rugby field. One could tell a man's general character pretty accurately from the way he scrummed down. Nunn had never seen Macintosh, Goldwasser, Rowe, or Riddle scrum down, but one could tell pretty well the way a man would scrum down from his general character.

Nunn could hardly have seen Riddle on a rugby field, of course, since she was a woman. Nunn thought about her carefully, and the longer he thought about her, the more she seemed to be the worst of the lot. In the records her name turned up increasingly often attached to undesirable minority opinions. Here she was opposing a recommendation that the Director's little girl should present the Queen with a bouquet. There she was arguing against the hiring of a red carpet and a canvas

63

awning to put outside the main entrance, against compulsory practice for all staff in official handshaking. The more detailed the arrangements for the royal visit became, the less effort she seemed to be making to hide her extraordinary opinions.

Then there was the strange business of the petition she had got up, the history of which was also documented in Sporting Records. There was the text of the petition itself, addressed to the Director, expressing alarm and anxiety about the preparations which were being made for the visit, and reminding Chiddingfold of the Institute's universal desire that the occasion should be an informal one. There was the confidential memorandum from Mrs. Plushkov to Nunn asking what he thought they should do about the petition, and Nunn's confidential reply to Mrs. Plushkov suggesting that the best thing to do at this stage was to go along with the protest movement and try to bring it out in the open. (Extraordinary advice. Who was this fellow Nunn, anyway? Perhaps *he* was ... Ah, hm, yes, of course. Jolly good.) Then there was the list of signatories. Riddle, Macintosh, Goldwasser, and Rowe at the top of the list, naturally. Then Mrs. Plushkov and Nunn, presumably added after their confidential consultation. Then Chiddingfold. (Chiddingfold! Something a little odd here, surely, in Chiddingfold signing a petition addressed to himself? Some touchingly human moment of misunderstanding, presumably. Perhaps he never descended far enough into the common world to read documents that were put before him for signature? Perhaps he never condescended to read anything? Perhaps he couldn't read?) After Chiddingfold everybody had signed it, and it had been presented to Chiddingfold, who had passed it to Nunn as Deputy Chairman of the Programme Committee, who was too busy with security work to deal with it himself, and who had passed it to the Secretary of the Programme Committee, Mrs. Plushkov, who minuted that the Committee had taken note of it and filed it for the record, where it came back to Nunn. Nunn examined it at great length, but found it exceedingly difficult to know how to evaluate it. He was greatly

64

struck by the fact that after he and Mrs. Plushkov had signed it to bring the bad security risks out into the open everyone else in the Institute had signed it. Did it mean that everyone was in fact a bad security risk? Or had everyone signed it because they thought they would seem bad security risks if they did *not* sign a petition which Nunn and Mrs. Plushkov had signed?

One thing was plain, anyway—the petition had been launched by Riddle, and anyone who launched a petition was certainly a grade one security risk. Nunn considered her carefully.

First of all she was scruffy, which was often a bad sign from the security point of view. Nunn made a note in his Horse of the Year Calendar. "1: Scruffy," he wrote. The more Nunn thought about her scruffiness, the more dangerous it seemed. Her hair always looked odd. Her shoes always needed heeling. A cigarette dangled permanently from her lips—a cigarette which she always referred to as a fag. As she always said, she was not a woman to mince her words. Perhaps, reflected Nunn thoughtfully, it was to avoid mincing her words that she always kept her fag in the extreme right-hand corner of her mouth. What should he write down to summarise his thinking here? "2. Haircut," he put.

"3," he wrote. What was the third most insecure thing about her? There was something he didn't much care for about her short-sightedness, and the thick spectacles she wore. Then again, the smoke from her fag perpetually made her eyes water, which presumably reduced her vision still further. And on top of that she had a hard smoker's cough which racked her incessantly, and which must have hopelessly shaken about what little she could see. "3," wrote Nunn. "Warped view of the world."

It was rumoured that she liked whisky. Well, everyone liked whisky. Nunn liked whisky. But then, Nunn was forced to admit to himself, he didn't wear pebble spectacles or have a cigarette which he called a fag dangling from the corner of his mouth. Then again, there was something vaguely improper about her. She might well have been described as an old maid. Yet her skirt rode up above her knees when she sat down. She frequently sat with her knees a foot or two apart, so that for ten or fifteen minutes at a time Nunn could see all the way up to her knickers, which were often apple green, or sky blue, or even black. Somewhere inside that run-down outer shell, one could not help feeling, there might be a naked, lustful woman still loose, and the gruff voice that rasped on about fags and loads of bloody balls might be shouting down the faint echo of some randy warbling from within. "4," wrote Nunn. "Immorality (?) leaves open to blackmail."

All in all, not a sound type. Nunn drew a box round her name in the Horse of the Year Calendar. He drew a scalloped edging round the box, then a box round the edging, and a line of loops round the new box, and a box round the loops. Then he surrounded the whole thing with a picture frame, and the picture frame with more boxing, scalloping, and loops, and the expanded version with another picture frame. Leaning very close to see what he was doing, he began to shade in the gaps between alternate sets of borders. One thing worried him as he worked. He knew for sure from his long years of dealing with subversion that anyone who got up a petition was merely acting as a front for some more sinister figure who remained unidentified. That was the man he really had to get at. Nunn turned over the possible names in his head. Rowe? Macintosh? Not nice names, certainly, but did they really have the authentic ring of treachery? What about Goldwasser? Goldwasser ... Goldwasser ... There was certainly something about that name—something that rang a bell, something that sounded not quite right, something unsound. Nothing definite, of course— just an old security man's little hunch.

Nunn added another to the list of Riddle's defects. "5. Goldwasser," he wrote.

15

Both Plushkov and Riddle spent a good deal of time in rallying support for their views on the official opening. It was difficult to see that they were having much effect. Plushkov's lobbying merely flattered those who were already antipathetic to subversive egalitarianism and Riddle. Riddle's efforts were ignored by everyone except those who already had honourable and ancient prejudices against royalty and Plushkov. There were only two exceptions to this general principle. One was Chiddingfold, who was tacitly recognised as a no man's land between the two factions, and the other was Haugh, the Head of the Fashion Department.

Haugh was a wonderfully responsive subject to lobbying. No lobbyist had ever come to him in vain. For a start he had no prejudices against anyone, not even the people almost everyone had prejudices against. He thought Nobbs was at heart sincere. He believed there was a great deal to be said for Goldwasser, and that Nunn had been much misunderstood. He said openly that it was not Macintosh's fault he was a Scotsman.

But above all, Haugh had an open mind. It was open at the front, and it was open at the back. Opinions, beliefs, philosophies entered, sojourned briefly, and were pushed out at the other end by the press of incoming convictions and systems. Lamarckism, Montanism, Leninism, Buchmanism, Kleinism, Spenglerism—they all blew in with the draught, whirled cheerfully around, and sailed out again. It depended on who had spoken to him last. On Tuesday morning he would meet a man who believed in acupuncture, cheap money, and hand-blocked Victorian wallpaper, and throughout the day he would go round with the sort of quiet, sincere devotion to these ideals that would clearly withstand torture and martyrdom. But on

Tuesday evening he would meet a man who pointed out that there were certain elementary logical flaws in the idea of acupuncture, cheap money, and hand-blocked Victorian wallpaper, and on Wednesday he would appear radiant with a gentle pity for all those naïve and credulous souls who had been taken in by them. "One has to work systematically," Rowe would say to him over coffee in the morning. "I know," Haugh would reply, his soft grey eyes filled with sincerity, and he would work systematically until lunch-time, when Macintosh would happen to remark to him over the soup: "System is the methodology of machines and fools." "I know," Haugh would reply, gently, so as not to make Macintosh feel how obvious his remark was. And he would work unsystematically all afternoon. He was a profoundly modest man, and in his modesty he knew that since he had evidently been wrong so often in the past, he was in no position now to cast stones at any idea, however wretched, or to refuse to take it in and give it shelter. His intelligence, unhampered by any critical processes, was quick and agile, and he was often convinced by a man's arguments before he had had time to put them. "I don't really think your theory stands up," someone would say to him. "I mean, if you look at all the evidence . . ."

"I know," Haugh would reply. "I know. It really doesn't stand up at all."

There was always a pleasant murmuring in the air at the Institute, and it was the sound of Haugh gently saying "I know." Everyone liked Haugh, since they found his ideas so congenial, and Haugh liked everyone, for much the same reasons.

Haugh's house was as open as his mind. People he had scarcely met called for meals, stayed on for the night, and remained for several months, quarrelling with one another and breaking the furniture, until they were dislodged by the press of new arrivals. Immense bottle parties occurred from time to time for no easily discernible reason, filling the house with repulsive people, or nice people pretending to be repulsive in order not to draw attention to themselves, and then ebbed again, as suddenly and inexplicably.

The Haughs' house, All Saints, was well adapted for this sort of treatment. It was a nineteenth-century neo-Gothic church, which Haugh and his wife had converted and decorated themselves. They cooked on a skilfully restored early Victorian range in the vestry, slept in witty antique sailors' hammocks in the north clerestory, and ate at the altar. They had hedged off the transepts with room-dividers and rubber plants to form from the north transept a play area and from the south a sun-loggia, though the brute glare of the noonday sun was somewhat softened by the time it had filtered through St. Arthur, St. Giles, St. Buryan, and St. Maud. The crypt was rented as a bed-sitter, and the whole of the nave left as an open-plan living-room. Running hot and cold water had been installed in the font.

The effect was heightened by the amusing objects with which the house was decorated—an old windlass, a Wimshurst machine, a bishop's cope, enamelled Victorian advertisements for stove-blacking and lucifers, a collection of Edwardian false teeth. Like the homeless layabouts and the many-splendoured cosmogonies, the cream of the world's junk-shops sought out Haugh's fabled hospitality. The stuff stayed long enough to get its breath back on the way down to limbo, and was then pushed out in favour of even more outrageous trouvailles.

One evening when a party seemed to be developing, Haugh was surprised and pleased to find that among the guests was almost the whole staff of the William Morris Institute. Conceivably someone had sent invitations out. Anyway, the occasion was a great success. Everyone gasped at the sight of All Saints, since they had not themselves managed to convert into houses anything more unsuitable than artisans' cottages, stables, or Salvation Army hostels. The font was turned into a punchbowl for the occasion, and the nave was soon completely filled with noise, as everyone spoke louder and louder to compete with the echo of the conversation booming vacantly back from the roof, until in most parts of the room hardly anyone could hear anything that anyone else was saying, which created the essential party feeling that wit and truth abounded on every hand, if only one could have heard them.

Plushkov hovered around Haugh, flattering him as best she could.

"One does think you've been terribly clever in converting this place," she mouthed inaudibly.

"I know," said Haugh, on the assumption that she had just put forward some new political or sociological theory.

"You!" cried Plushkov, whose well-modulated feminine voice was incapable of rising above a certain discreet level of output. "Clever!"

"I know. He is, tremendously," said Haugh admiringly, greatly impressed by Ewe's work already.

Chiddingfold and his wife arrived and came among their subjects. They stood like two immense ice-puddings, towering, massive, immobile, freezing everything within range. Chiddingfold seemed to be trying to shrink into himself, as if to deprecate the vastness of his authority and to become as other men for the evening. From somewhere inside that great fortress a small man looked out, smiling as best a prisoner might, amazingly conversational for a man who has spent so long in solitary confinement. "Hallo," he said to anyone who came near enough, and smiled shyly.

Goldwasser found himself alongside.

"Hallo," said Chiddingfold.

"Good evening, Director," said Goldwasser.

Chiddingfold smiled. Goldwasser smiled. There was nothing more to be said. But something more *had* to be said, felt Goldwasser. They were standing as if in conversation. Some sort of conversation, however minimal, had to occur. Chiddingfold's eyes sank slowly until they rested on the undemanding mid-parts of people in the middle distance, the remains of his smile still lingering about his lips like crumbs left over from a cold snack. Goldwasser looked desperately about him, hunting for a usable topic. Art? Politics? Sociology? He couldn't think of anything to say about any of them. He couldn't remember the name of a single artist of any sort, or a single fashionable political or sociological question. His mental processes were paralysed, numbed by the waves of cold that emanated from Chiddingfold in spite of all Chiddingfold's efforts. Goldwasser examined the contents of his glass at great length, and then drank from it slowly and thoughtfully. It had been empty for some time.

"Well," he said finally, "at least we can all say we've been to church this week-end."

Chiddingfold's blue eyes rested on Goldwasser for a moment. Something registered in their depths, some small private agony. His smile deepened to its polite maximum, then slackened again to its minimum position. They had had a conversation, thought Goldwasser, so now at last the interview could be decently terminated.

"I must be getting along," he said. Chiddingfold smiled again, absently, as if at a family joke which touched some remote nostalgia in him. Goldwasser waited for a few moments, and then moved away with great definiteness, as if he were answering an urgent call for his services.

Elsewhere the uproar continued. Some of the guests who were not from the Institute were audibly resentful of those who were.

"Who are all these people?" they shouted at one another.

"All which people?"

"All these tits in tweed sports jackets."

"I believe they're from some sort of institution."

"What are they doing here, then?"

"Friends of Haugh's, I'm told."

"Peculiar friends he has."

"Tits, a lot of them."

"They're just standing around talking to one another."

"I know. Spoil the party, rather."

"Yes."

Rowe was shouting shop to Haugh in one of the spots where acoustics were bad.

"My personal view . . ." his words came through, ". . . wher-ever . . . decisions . . . finite range of possible alternatives . . . can be done by a computer . . ."

"That's right," shouted Haugh.

"I personally . . . good idea . . . programme . . . write porno-graphic . . ."

"I know. What did you say?"

"Pornographic novels."

"I know."

"And . . ."

"Exactly."

"And sex manuals."

"I know. I know."

People kept going up to Mrs. Plushkov and asking if her hus-band was at the party.

". . . think . . . here somewhere," she replied.

". . . always *died* . . ."

"Oh, no . . . very much alive . . ."

"No, I always have . . . to meet him."

Nunn was in great form. He was giving Mrs. Haugh a clear analysis of the performance of each member of the English International XV throughout the season. He realised that Mrs. Haugh knew nothing about rugby, and so was kindly provid-ing a sort of simultaneous interpretation of everything he said into terms of association football. It occurred to him that she knew nothing about association football either, but there were limits to what he could do to entertain his fellow creatures. Nobody could say, said Nunn to himself, that he did not put himself out to be pleasant to even the weirdest people. Jokes he was providing—and explaining—in his jolliest and sauciest manner. But by God, if Mrs. Haugh didn't stop looking past him with that trapped, haggard look he would put her name down in his Official Badminton Diary as sure as God made little apples.

Goldwasser was a little tight—tight enough to marvel at the skill with which he was concealing the fact. He could only see what was straight in front of his eyes, like a horse with blinkers, and this limitation of his field of vision seemed to concentrate his mental powers wonderfully. He got the pulpit in his sights, and the absurdity of finding a pulpit at a party was profoundly and uniquely revealed to him. He couldn't help smiling at it. He couldn't stop smiling at it.

A little later he found Plushkov in front of him. She was talking to him, quite inaudibly, and her eyes, her eyebrows, and the lines around her mouth exquisitely emphasised the unheard points. To Goldwasser she seemed remote, as if he were seeing her through the wrong end of a telescope. He was filled with pity for her. Every well-formed smile, every graceful lift of her eyebrows, seemed to delineate an intolerable sadness.

"Oh, Plushkov, Plushkov, Plushkov!" he heard himself sighing.

"I beg your pardon?" she queried inaudibly.

"OH, PLUSHKOV!" he roared.

She smiled with polite incomprehension.

"So interesting," she said.

He yearned to encourage her in some way.

"Your eyes are beautiful," he said. "Your goodness of soul shows in your eyes."

"I beg your pardon?" she said.

"BEAUTIFUL EYES!" he shouted. She looked puzzled.

"GOOD TEETH!" he roared. "NICE LEGS!"

He took her hand and pressed it.

"Oh, Plushkov," he said. "I worship you from afar. WORSHIP YOU! ME! I DO! FROM AFAR!"

Plushkov disengaged her hand swiftly and disappeared into the outer confusion of his field of vision. When he saw her again she was saying something to Mrs. Haugh and both of them were looking in his direction. Mrs. Haugh seemed very anxious about something.

In the north transept Haugh was explaining his philosophy of life to Mrs. Rowe.

"My personal view," he was shouting, "is that we have to

take a decision on what to do with computers. There's an infinite range of possible alternatives, but I personally think the choice lies between pornographic novels and sex manuals."

"What?" cried Mrs. Rowe.

"PORNOGRAPHIC NOVELS AND SEX MANUALS."

"What about them?"

"WHETHER WE SHOULD WRITE THEM BY COMPUTER."

"Write them by computer? What on earth for?"

"I know. I know. There's no earthly reason at all."

Mrs. Macintosh was stuck with Nobbs. He had trapped her against a table of refreshments, and every time she made as if to move away, he snatched up the peanuts, the crisps, or the cheez-ee-twiggees, and thrust them in front of her, barring her progress. Every now and then he would charitably toss her an observation on the scene.

"Funny-looking lot of people, aren't they?" he would shout.

"What's funny about them?" Mrs. Macintosh would shout back, trying for humanitarian reasons to save the life of any infant conversation, no matter how unappealing it seemed.

"I don't know. They just look a funny lot." After a while he would have another go.

"To me, that is," he would shout. "But then maybe I've just got funny ideas."

To keep himself going through the long watches between remarks he sucked up frequent handfuls of peanuts. There were two peanuts nesting companionably in his beard. When he had exhausted the subject of the company he turned his attention to the fabric.

"Weird-looking place this is," he shouted. "Looks more like a church than a house to me."

"I believe it used to be one," shouted Mrs. Macintosh.

"Well, that's what it looks like," confirmed Nobbs graciously. "To me."

Goldwasser got Chiddingfold in his sights again. "Hallo," said Chiddingfold, with exactly the same note of implausible surprise as before. "Good evening, Director," said Goldwasser.

His heart sank. Conversation was going to have to be made, which was difficult enough in itself, without letting it become apparent to those percipient blue eyes that one was very slightly pooped. He cast wildly about for a topic, but all the topics in the world seemed to dart away from his narrow beam of vision and lose themselves in the roaring confusion at the sides. He held up his empty glass and looked at the light through it judicially for a long time.

"Well," he said at last with great care, "first party I've been to after which one is able to give as an excuse that one was in church."

Chiddingfold's smile increased briefly and subsided again. There, thought Goldwasser, I've done it. Perfectly easy. He made his way back to the font quite cheerfully.

In the south chancel Mrs. Haugh was consulting Mrs. Nunn.

"Never know . . . what one should do . . ."

"What should one do?"

"I never know . . ."

"What?"

"About Goldwasser . . . very drunk . . ."

"Very drunk? Goldwasser?"

"According to Mrs. Plushkov he . . . then . . . and grabbed hold of her."

"Goldwasser? Attacked Mrs. Plushkov?"

"And said . . . terrible things . . ."

"Foul language, I suppose."

". . . legs . . ."

"By the legs?"

"And then . . . teeth . . ."

"His teeth? Sank them into her? Bit her?"

"Oh . . . must feel very bitter."

Macintosh stood in the pulpit, leaning ponderously on the rail as if he were on his gantry, and gazing abstractedly at all the perambulating ethical machines in the room, perhaps wondering which of them would go overboard to save a sandbag. Goldwasser stood beneath and gazed up at him.

"Someone ought to go and save my wife from Nobbs," shouted Macintosh. "But the point is, Goldwasser, I've been drinking. I mean, thinking. Freudian slip there, Goldwasser. The point is, Goldwasser, are you really cleverer than me?"

"I'm not sure, Macintosh. I think so."

"I suppose you are. Do you ever worry about it?"

"Yes."

"So do I. But listen, Goldwasser, I think you're so bloody clever that you can see just how limited your cleverness is. Now the thing about me is that I'm so stupid I can't understand how stupid I am."

"I know."

"So that effectively I may possibly be cleverer than you. Do you take my point?"

"Oh, I thought of it a long time ago."

"Aha. You thought of it, and then immediately doubted it?"

"Of course."

"Your cleverness is self-destructive, Goldwasser."

"What an obvious thing to say, Macintosh! Christ, you're such a lump, Macintosh, such a slow-witted, mulish, insensitive juggins! If you knew how you irritated me sometimes!"

They gazed about them, pleased with themselves.

"Such an appalling exhibition," said Mrs. Nunn to Mrs. Chiddingfold. "Now ... shouting abuse at Macintosh ... two minutes ago ... indecent assault ... poor Queenie Plushkov ..."

The party was becoming a little quieter, as more and more topics of conversation were finally run to earth and battered to death. Plushkov, who was standing with Nunn, found her voice was becoming audible again.

"I'm not sure whether one has managed to make any headway with Haugh or not," she said.

"Or not what?" said Nunn.

"Headway. With Haugh."

"Have you? Jolly good."

"He's got some extraordinary idea into his head about

76

getting the Institute to run a programme for pornographic novels and sex manuals."

"For what?"

"Pornographic novels and sex manuals."

Nunn stiffened. Pornographic novels and sex manuals! Raising their ugly heads again! Had he so skilfully extirpated this nonsense in Macintosh only to see it springing up again in Plushkov? It was like an underground fire, bursting out where one least expected it. Well, Plushkov needn't think that the patronage she had enjoyed from him in the past would protect her from having her name written down in a sporting diary now.

"Jolly good," he said absently. "So that's your idea, is it?"

"Not mine. Haugh's."

Haugh's. Of course, he might have guessed it. An unreliable man, Haugh, a weak link in the team. He would take his name. In fact he could consider it taken already.

"Though knowing Haugh," said Plushkov, "One doesn't suppose he thought it up himself."

"I beg your pardon?"

"Just repeating it—Haugh. Somebody else must have thought of it."

"Somebody else? Who?"

"One doesn't know. But judging by his behaviour to-night I shouldn't put it past Goldwasser."

"I beg your pardon?"

"GOLDWASSER!"

Goldwasser! So it was Goldwasser at the bottom of all this pornography! Of course it was Goldwasser. It was Goldwasser who skulked about in the Heads of Departments urinal. It was Goldwasser who had put Riddle up to her petition. One look at Goldwasser and you could see he was a trouble-maker, a barrack-room lawyer, a man with a chip on his shoulder. Nunn had met his type before.

He got out his diary. Under 3 March it said Goldwasser. Under 5 December and 17 August and 23 January—Goldwasser.

Under Memo—Goldwasser. Under National Insurance Number—Goldwasser. Under Size in Football Boots, Law Terms, Record Breaks at Billiards—Goldwasser, Goldwasser, Goldwasser. The evidence was all there. It was amazing that he had not seen it before. He wrote his conclusions down succinctly and damningly inside the back cover, thus: GOLDWASSER.

The party was beginning to reach its end. There was a last stir, as people moved around to thank the hosts, or to say hallo to people they had not been able to bear to say hallo to earlier. Goldwasser moved out from his refuge in the chancel, and found himself at once undeniably face to face with Chiddingfold.

"Hallo," said Chiddingfold, neither less nor more surprised, neither less nor more enthusiastic, than before.

"Good evening, Director," said Goldwasser. His mind reeled helplessly. He could not hold three conversations with Chiddingfold in one evening! It was not within the range of human endurance. For a moment he believed he would be able to turn wordlessly and run lightly out of the house. Then he believed he might be able to fall down in a dead faint. But secretly he knew all the time he would have to stand and deliver. He looked down into his glass, and swirled the non-existent contents round, then rolled them round his mouth and swallowed them noisily. He wondered wildly whether Chiddingfold even knew he was the same person, or whether his mind was not so far removed from the particular that he could not distinguish between one human being and another anyway. One thing was certain, though; this time he must think of a fresh topic of conversation.

"As a natural Whig," he said with a sad elaborate whimsicality, "I'm afraid I view with what can only be described as mixed feelings the prospect of telling my grandchildren that I was once a member of this great church party."

Even as he said it he realised it was the same joke. He did not dare watch the exhausted waxing and waning of

78

Chiddingfold's mirthless smile. But he did not have to, for at that moment there was a diversion. Riddle emerged. But a transformed Riddle—a smiling Riddle with pink cheeks and glowing sleepy eyes. Where she had been no one knew, but what she had been doing was plain enough. She put her arms round Chiddingfold's neck, and gesturing largely towards the eastern end of the house, sang:

> "Walter, Walter!
> Lead me to the altar!
> It's either the workhouse or you."

There was a horrified, enthralled silence. For a moment everyone paused in mid-handshake, or with overcoat half on to shoulders. To see Chiddingfold drunkenly assaulted was delicious horror enough, but to hear a Christian name postulated for him sent a delectable shiver down even the strongest spine. Then Riddle tried to move, apparently with the object of dragging Walter to the altar, and the two of them fell heavily to the floor still clasped together. The last thing Goldwasser saw before responsible citizens rushed in to raise the wreck was Chiddingfold's face, still articulating no complaint, still firmly locked in its polite, embarrassed smile.

16

Riddle was not easily abashed, but when she thought about her indecent assault upon Chiddingfold she felt something that was definitely less than aplomb. When she thought about it at home, among the comforting shambles of books, fag packets, and old fag ends in her flat—a huge empty Victorian room suitable for accommodating forty people each eighteen feet tall, or one Riddle and the copious offscourings of her daily life—it seemed to her that it was just the sort of laughable little incident in which any good party abounded. But when she thought about it at work, in the somehow more alien shambles of books, fag packets, and old fag ends in her laboratory at the Institute, she did feel something that was undeniably abashment. Assault— all right. Anyone might leap on someone in an unguarded moment. But on Chiddingfold! Why had she had to pick Chiddingfold?

She could no longer remember exactly what she had had in mind when she emerged from behind the pulpit and caught sight of Chiddingfold smiling his small social smile. She could not recall quite whether she had felt an urgent desire to love or to mock that great-headed, polite, vulnerable-impregnable totem. Or whether she felt both. Or whether she had thought for a moment that they were almost the same thing.

Anyway, she felt a certain relief when one of her laboratory assistants told her that Goldwasser had launched some sort of assault on Mrs. Plushkov at the same party. Dear old Goldwasser! At least she wasn't the only person in the Institute with normal sexual vitality. The more she thought about Goldwasser the more surprised she was that she had not realised he was a sexual dynamo before. He was so gentle and nervous and considerate—the paradox cried out for completion.

She felt a touch of jealousy that Goldwasser had chosen to assault Mrs. Plushkov rather than her. A great prurient curiosity—or a great tenderness—seized her, and one afternoon when she knew he would be alone, she called on Goldwasser in his laboratory.

"Well," she wheezed, perching provocatively on the corner of his desk and tilting her head back to keep the cigarette smoke out of her eyes, "how's tricks, Goldwasser, old cock?"

"Fine," said Goldwasser.

"Hope you don't mind being all alone with the local scarlet woman?"

"Who's that?"

"Me, old son."

"You?"

"Can't conceal it any more after that party."

"Oh. No. I mean, well . . ."

"Don't mince your words, buddy boy. I'm practically the local Messalina."

"Oh. I see."

Goldwasser tried to lean back in his chair as if casually. Every time Riddle coughed, the ash from her cigarette fell intimately into his lap.

"Anyway," she said, "we ought to stick together."

"Who?"

"You and me."

"Oh. Well, yes."

"Birds of a feather."

"What?"

"Tarred with the same brush, old lad."

"Ah."

Goldwasser was not entirely with her. Everyone in the Institute knew that Goldwasser had assaulted Mrs. Plushkov except Goldwasser. Out of a tactful regard for his feelings, nobody had told him.

81

"It's a funny thing really, old son," said Riddle, resting her foot on the arm of Goldwasser's chair, so that her knee came level with his face, "that we've never really joined forces."

"H'm."

"Don't you think it's a bit bloody peculiar?"

"Well . . . yes . . . I mean . . ."

Goldwasser was finding it increasingly difficult not to see that Riddle's stocking had two ladders in it above the knee, and that her underwear was tangerine-coloured. He didn't want to think unjustly of anyone, but he couldn't help remembering Riddle's assault on Chiddingfold. He struggled with an unworthy feeling of panic.

"I mean," said Riddle, "I hope you don't mind my talking like this?"

"No."

"You know me. I always call a spade a bleeding spade."

"Yes."

"And after all, we do have something in common."

"Oh?"

"Well, don't we?"

"Do we?"

Goldwasser was hypnotised by the tiny white discs of Riddle's knee that kept appearing, as flakes of hot ash from her cigarette melted her nylon stocking just in front of his nose. He felt like a mesmerised rabbit. He had a sudden presentiment that in the next few seconds she would leap on him, as she had on Chiddingfold, singing a ribald song, and drag him to the floor. Tearing his eyes away from the scene on the knee, he jumped urgently to his feet and stared about him for some excuse to escape.

God Almighty! thought Riddle with a mainly awful shock of terror, this great volcanic monosyllabic brute is going to attack me exactly here and now!

She was instantly overcome by a prolonged spasm of coughing. Psychosomatic, she thought to herself, as the fag-end shot out of her mouth and fell in the waste-paper basket. She and

Goldwasser were still spreading the contents out over the floor searching for it when Nobbs came in, holding a file.

"If I'm not interfering in your private life, mate," he said to Goldwasser, "perhaps you'd tell me when, if ever, you propose to make a decision on 'Paralysed Girl Determined to Dance Again.'"

"Now!" cried Goldwasser. "Don't go, Nobbs. Draw up a chair, Nobbs."

Later Goldwasser felt that he had been stupidly wrong about the whole incident, and became convinced that Riddle had intended nothing but a friendly conversation. He went round to her laboratory to set things on a better footing, but found her out. Looking round the seedy confusion in the room to make sure that Riddle was not somewhere amongst it, his eye was caught by a birthday card, covered with cherubs and golden bells and glitter dust, which was standing on the console of the department's Ajax IV computer. Inside it was written:

To my own darling little Ajax.

You're a naughty boy at times, but all is forgiven 'cos you're one year old to-day. ,

With lots of love and kisses,

From

Mummy

To neither of these incidents did either Riddle or Goldwasser ever subsequently refer.

17

Rowe shelved his novel about Lisbeth and Howard until he had had time to read the subject up a bit in an *Encyclopædia of Sexual Deviations* he had bought. In the meantime he started work on a straightforward comic novel called *Take A Bloke Like Me.*

"It's nothing, really," he told Goldwasser one afternoon when he dropped in to see how things were going. "It's just about, well, perfectly ordinary chaps."

"Like you and me?" said Goldwasser.

"Exactly. There's nothing special about them. There are four of them, and they just drink beer, and try to lay this perfectly ordinary girl. She's called Annie Crumpet."

"What are they called? Graham Standish, Patrick Melhuish, Dick Cornish, and Jim Parrish?"

"No—Patrick Cornish, Jim Standish, Dick Parrish and Graham Melhuish. Would you like to read it?"

"It's finished, is it?"

"No. I've just done the first seduction scene so far. I thought I'd write all the seduction scenes first and then fill in the rest afterwards."

"That's ingenious."

"Anyway, in this one Graham Cornish—no, I mean, Patrick Parrish—has taken Annie back to his bed-sitter. I hope you can read the writing. I mean, you're not forced to stagger through it if you don't want to."

"No."

"But if you'd really like to . . ."

"Oh, of course."

"I mean, tell me what you think of it."

Goldwasser took the manuscript and read:

Graham made a noise which sounded remarkably like the bath-water running out of a particularly dirty-minded plug-hole. Annie was not sure that she liked it. It put her in mind of the noises made by the geyser in the bathroom at home. That was emphatically *not* something she wished to be reminded about just at present, thank you. She did her best to pretend not to have heard.

"My God," said Graham, "they shouldn't let girls like you loose. They really shouldn't. You agree to come up to a bloke's room, and then you come over all hard-to-get, while the poor bloke or chap, in this case yours truly, languishes with his tongue hanging out."

"What's wrong with that?" asked Annie, sitting down on the sofa as far away from Graham as she could without appearing to be prim.

"What's wrong with it?" yelped Graham. "I'll get a cold in my tongue, that's what's wrong with it, young lady."

She could not repress a small gerk of laughter at this. There was definitely something endearing about Dick's sense of humour, she decided, even though he was Not the Sort of Young Man One Could Take Home to One's Parents, and was very probably just about to say something pretty off-putting like: 'You Do Something to Me, Baby.' His hand, she realised, was already moseying along the sofa in the general direction of her right knee. She picked it up with the idea of chasing it off the premises, and found that Dick had put in a spot of overtime during the diversion and got his other arm round her shoulders. Having Graham's arm round one's shoulders, she decided, was definitely nice.

"You're a hot bit of stuff," he breathed, nuzzling her ear for good measure.

It was funny, she reflected, how many men had tried to nuzzle her ear and tell her, slavering appreciatively about the chops, that she was a hot bit of stuff. She certainly had small, high breasts and nice legs. There must be a bull market in small, high breasts, she decided, and realised that Jim's hand, which had up till now been putting in some solid spadework on her left shoulder, was now shuffling hopefully down towards one of the said small, high landmarks.

"No," she said as firmly as she could. She felt mean, but how could she explain that though she usually let boys she particularly liked, after a reasonably plush evening out, get about as far as Camp Five on one of the small, high properties already catalogued, she always insisted on his going the proper way about it. The proper way about it, as far as she was concerned, was arm round shoulders, kiss, stroke back, hand inside blouse and stroke back inside, *then* bash on to the breast.

"Oh, God," groaned Patrick. "Back to square one. Every time I go up even the tiniest ladder I find there's a ruddy great snake waiting at the top. What's on your mind, young lady? Don't you *like* normal healthy relations between blokes and blokesses? Do you think there's something *wrong* with a healthy dollop of good old British snogging?"

"Oh, no," she said quickly. "I think it's nice. It's just that there's a Right and a Wrong Way of Going About It."

"Oh, God," groaned Graham. "You're not going to give me that stuff about your precious virginity, are you? Because you know where you can stuff that, don't you? Where the monkey put his nuts."

She snorted involuntarily. She could not be angry for long with a man who wooed her with jokes like that. She let him put his arm round her again. It was nice, she decided. She did not even raise any objection when, after a decent interval had elapsed, he began to push through a tentative programme of ear-nibbling, back-stroking, and knee-fingering. Having her ear nibbled was a nice sensation. She had a nice feeling in her back and her knee.

"I've knocked about a bit in my time," he breathed, "but cross my heart and hope to die, I'll tell you something I've never told anyone else in the world—you're the real cat's pyjamas, sweetie. No kidding."

He kissed her, and the kiss seemed to go on for about a million years. A curious sensation ran through her that for a moment she couldn't find a word to describe. Then, when his lips took off for a brief holiday from the job in hand, she realised what it was.

"That was nice," she said.

A moment later she could feel a dirty great hand fumbling with the moorings of the good ship brassière.

"Sorry, cobber," she said, regretfully hoisting herself into the vertical. "But this is where you and I definitely come to the parting of the ways."

"Oh, God," cried Dick disgustedly. "I thought all this sort of balls went out with button boots!"

"That's as far as I've got at the moment," said Rowe, as Goldwasser laid the manuscript down.

"Nice," said Goldwasser.

"No, seriously, tell me what you think of it."

"Very nice."

"Be more specific."

"Well, I just think it's, well, *nice*."

"No, come on. Be frank. Don't be afraid of hurting my feelings."

"All right. I think it's very forthright."

"Forthright?"

"I mean, the action raging back and forth between forthright discussion of the pros and cons of premarital intercourse and forthright horseplay among the suspenders and shoulder-straps. I liked the idea. It's very—well, it's very forthright."

"I'm glad you think that. I must say I think it is real life."

"And the language is very—well, very *forthright*, isn't it?"

"I think so. And pretty fresh, isn't it?"

"Oh, very fresh. Fresh without being offensive, I thought. It did away with all those rather provocative overtones the subject sometimes has."

"Well, yes . . ."

"And the portrayal of character is marvellous. What happens in the end?"

"Well, Patrick . . ."

"No, I can guess. Patrick gets tight at a party. Annie gets him on his own in the bedroom, and keeps on and on at him, and finally he has to give in because he's too exhausted to go on struggling."

"No, you see . . ."

"So she makes him take off his cloak of facetiousness, and all his saucy under-facetiousness, and has her way with him—makes him speak two straight words one after another. It's painful for a moment, but once it's over he's rather glad."

"I take the point, Goldwasser, but . . ."

"Annie enjoys a moment of intense pleasure, of course. But it was chasing him back through all those layers of gangling verbiage that she really enjoyed. It's a sad story, Rowe, but I have to admit that it has the salty savour of real life."

18

There were now thirty committees, and between them they had gone approximately thirty times as far towards planning an informal occasion that She would like as one of the committees would have done on its own. When individual members stopped to think about it, they were sometimes a little surprised at exactly how far they *had* gone. It would not have occurred to any of them individually that what She would like would be to have all the gentlemen's lavatories boarded up, but to the committees this had been transparently obvious. If Rowe, say, or Goldwasser, had been making the plans in their capacity as Rowe or Goldwasser it would not have struck them that the occasion would scarcely be a truly informal one unless twelve hundred square feet of turf were hired and laid down in the asphalt courtyard for the afternoon to turn it into an informal garden. But to the committees this went without saying.

The more Goldwasser thought about it, the more surprised he was at the corporate effect produced by Macintosh, Rowe, Riddle, and Haugh, who after all formed an effective majority of the committees' membership. The more Macintosh thought about it, the more surprised *he* was at the corporate nature of Haugh, Riddle, Rowe, and Goldwasser. Rowe, Haugh, and Riddle entertained similar astonishment.

For a start they had formed something of a democratic bloc. But Macintosh had entirely lost interest in the whole question after two meetings. Goldwasser remained interested in theory, but could not make his mind run slow enough to remain in contact with the actual progress of the committees' business, and over and over again found himself emerging from a day-dream about the cube root of the speed of light to hear Mrs. Plushkov saying: ". . . take that as generally agreed? Minute it, then, will you, Miss Fram?" Haugh, of course, could always see the force of the other side's arguments, and Riddle, it was felt, was becoming a little *boring* in her vociferous opposition to everything. Depressed by the Chiddingfold incident, and by the somewhat ambiguous state in which her relations with Goldwasser had been left by the events around the waste-paper basket, she even felt she was boring herself.

And Rowe's views were changing. It was no longer totally obvious to him that it was ludicrous to erect crush-barriers outside the Institute and assemble local crowds to put behind them. If, he began to think, the people who got things done *did* in fact get things done they could not be the fools that people who did *not* have to get things done sometimes took them for. If they got things done they must be fairly sound and reasonable people. And if they were fairly sound and reasonable people, the things they got done must be fairly sound and reasonable things to do.

The whole field of arguments both For and Against had always seemed to him to be incredibly confused. He wasn't *exactly* sure, he realised when he put a snap question to himself in the middle of the night, *what* the arguments were for and against. He couldn't see exactly where the arguments for left off and the arguments against started. Or rather, he could see some of the arguments on both sides. Or to be even more precise, he could *almost* see some of the arguments on both sides.

The only thing he could see with absolute clarity in this wild lunar landscape was himself. There he stood, he could see, making sense of the terrible complexities around him with a hard intellectual pertinacity and an engaging modesty. "Devastating analysis of the problems of our time," said the extracts from the reviews that seemed to hang in the sky above the chaos below. "A refreshing ability to go straight to the heart of the matter." "Here is a man who refuses to be fooled."

Around this sharply-etched central figure other, slightly less well-defined faces could be discerned among the tangled thickets of argument. Macintosh, Plushkov, Chiddingfold, Nunn—they all looked to him hopefully for a lead. He found himself backing away from the thickets containing Riddle and Goldwasser. There was something about them . . . well, something that didn't exactly inspire confidence. Not their sexual eccentricities, of course. It could scarcely be that, seeing that he was a man of whom the reviewers had written—or would write, as soon as the opportunity arose—"His broad understanding of the world of human nature is proverbial." There were enough small high breasts in his novel to guarantee his broad-mindedness on that score. But there was something about them that was not quite sound. Those petitions that Riddle put about, for instance. Not really the sort of thing sound people did. And Goldwasser. It was difficult to pin down exactly what he objected to about Goldwasser. He had an intuitive feeling that he was not a very good judge of literature. Then again, there was something rather flippant about him. He was a man whose loyalty to his friends could not in certain circumstances be relied on. Well, to put it rather crudely, he was not a man to whom one would want to show, say, a book on which one was working.

Anyway, when the time came to vote on the proposal to paint imaginary curtains in the windows of the disused storeroom at the back of the International Affairs Department, Macintosh failed to turn up, Goldwasser never heard what the proposal was, Riddle said scarcely enough against it for Haugh to agree with her even temporarily, and Rowe consciously and deliberately voted in favour.

He felt a sense of release at his decision. At last he was shaking off the fetters of youth and leaving irresponsibility behind. At last he was becoming a sound man.

19

Where on earth does one buy a pair of ceremonial gold tape-cutting scissors? The Protocol Committee did not know, and asked the Sub-Committee on Ceremonial. The Sub-Committee on Ceremonial turned in bewilderment to the Joint Advisory Committee on Protocol and Ceremonial, and the Joint Advisory Committee on Protocol and Ceremonial, on Haugh's advice, asked Haugh.

Haugh rapidly found a magazine called *Ceremonial Ware News*, and from the advertisements there selected a firm called the Empire Ceremonial Supply Company Limited, which looked as if it catered for the better-class trade, and was a member of the Ceremonial Waremongers' Fidelity Guarantee Scheme.

"Ceremonial golden scissors?" said the manager when Haugh visited their showrooms. "Certainly, sir. Made-to-measure? Or can I show you something from our comprehensive range of ready-to-use ware? They're very popular in these busy days.

"What had you in mind, sir? Rolled gold, gold plate, silver gilt, or solid gold? Chased, jewelled, or plain? Did you want left-handed or right-handed? Now, as far as length goes I can do you anything from six inches to twenty-eight inches. If you want anything outside that I'm afraid they'll have to be specially made.

"Now here's rather a nice model, sir. This is the Sandringham. A very nice scissor—a very nice scissor, indeed. Perhaps you'd like to hold it, sir. Do you feel how snugly it sits in the hand? Try it on this demonstration tape here ... that's right, sir. Lovely action, isn't it?

"Or perhaps you'd prefer something more traditional? Have

a look at the Osborne. A very conservative scissor, this one. I expect some people would think it was a bit old-fashioned, but as a matter of fact we sell quite a lot of them. Oh, yes, there's something about tradition, isn't there, sir, whatever they say . . .

"This one, sir? This is the Holyrood. It's a heavy-duty scissor for the thicker tape. You'll find some of your big contractors and engineering firms put up a very heavy gauge tape if you don't watch them.

"Now this one's the Balmoral. *Very* fashionable now, sir. More what they call the Italian cut. It's a very smart piece of scissoring, sir—in tremendous demand among the younger set.

"Of course, if you have a budget to bear in mind—and who hasn't, these days?—you might prefer to invest in a used pair. Yes, of course. Would you step this way, sir? We have a very representative stock of guaranteed used ware. It has of course all been serviced in our own workshops. I beg your pardon, sir? Oh, the original inscriptions removed, sir. Not at all, sir, not at all. A very sensible question.

"The used scissors are in these cases over here. I don't know whether you're interested in anything else? Golden hammers? Silver trowels? Ceremonial switches? Certainly, sir, the switches are along this wall here. How about that big one at the back? It was formerly used by the Duchess of Middlesex to open the new Whuish hydro-electric scheme. What had you in mind exactly, sir . . . ? Computers? Perhaps this one with the gold-plated condensers would be rather suitable. We built it on the premises here for Miss Romaine Roxy to switch on the illuminations at Weston-super-Mare. Then it was used again for the illuminations at South Shields, with the Lord Lieutenant of Durham officiating, if I remember correctly. It's seen a bit of life, that switch, sir.

"As a matter of fact I often think to myself 'If only some of these things could talk, what a tale they'd have to tell!' I mean, take that little hammer with the ivory handle over there, sir. It's a special lightweight model made for the Dowager Marchioness of Menai, when she was laying the foundation stone of the new gymnasium at her old school. She's very frail, you know. Or look at that golden spade in the corner. That was used by Lord Frome to plant a memorial oak in the Fellows' Garden at the Andover Presbyterian Seminary in 1927. He was eighty-four at the time, and he rose from his sick-bed to do it. And within a week, sir, he was—dead.

"Think of the doors that have been opened with these golden keys, sir! Think of all the cakes these ceremonial swords have cut! Incidentally, sir, if you see anything you would like demonstrated we have a demonstration theatre fully equipped with a foundation stone, a cake, a ship's prow . . .

"That, sir? That's the gold-plated starting-pistol with which Sir Robert Gumble started the Mandated Territories Games in 1936 . . . That's the silver microphone through which Rock Richmond sang the thousandth song published by the Cathedral Music Publishing Company . . . the silver corkscrew used by General Sir Roderick Talltrouser at the bicentenary of Brown's Club . . . the silver-gilt penny with which Horace Walpole inaugurated Croydon's new public lavatories in 1921 . . . the solid gold starting-handle with which the King of Rumania started the first Austin Seven to be sold in Bucharest . . . the diamond fuse-pin out of the grenade with which Mussolini opened the invasion of Abyssinia . . ."

Haugh was entranced. He ordered the "Balmoral" scissors, a jewelled switch, a silver-gilt trowel, a length of golden chain of unspecified purpose, a golden key, and a gas-fired golden taper with which ex-Princess Beatrice of Swabia once lit a flame of undying remembrance to the cows and sheep which fell gloriously in the municipal abattoir at West Wandsworth.

94

20

When he was tired and teleological, Goldwasser sometimes believed he could discern a purpose in Nobbs's existence. It was to keep him, Goldwasser, in his place by counterbalancing the inherent simplicity of his work in the Newspaper Department, compared with that of his colleagues in all the other departments.

They were all handicapped by the fact that even the biggest known computer has only a fraction of the capacity and complexity of the human brain. Goldwasser was not. The human brains he was replacing, he discovered as he analysed the newspaper files, suffered from neither capacity nor complexity. Or if they did, they didn't let it interfere with their work. As if foreseeing the limited intellects of the digital computers which would one day replace them, they had introduced the most drastic simplifications into their work already.

There was no need for Goldwasser to waste the limited stock of storage circuits at his disposal by programming the computer to deal with cortisone, streptomycin, cyclizine, sulphaphenyltrimethylaminodiazine, carbolic acid, and aspirin. "Wonder drug" did for all of them. The need for Kensington, Westminster, Holborn, Paddington, Hammersmith, and Edgware was conveniently satisfied by the one word "Mayfair." One of the biggest and most heterogeneous ranges of subject was replaced by one of the shortest words; pornography, marriage, indecent exposure, love, sodomy, birth, tenderness, striptease, etc., etc., were all "sex."

On this principle, therefore, it was unnecessary to struggle to programme a computer whose range included writing stories about, say:—

A man at Notting Hill Gate who claims to have reduced

teenage delinquency by showing lantern slides about development in puberty;

An acquittal for a man accused of indecent exposure in a park at Ealing;

A Gloucester Road man who is unhurt after slipping on a manhole cover outside the Shakespeare Memorial Theatre while Romeo and Juliet is being performed;

An elderly businessman from Maida Vale whose arthritis clears up almost exactly four years after a visit to a strip club.

All the computer had to write was:—

MAYFAIR MAN IN SEX SHOW MIRACLE.

There were other simplifications, too, that made Goldwasser's life easier. A man who manufactured shoe polish, or marketed shoe polish, or appeared in television commercials for shoe polish, or organised a strike against the shoe-polish manufacturers, or ate shoe polish, was simply "Mr. Shoe Polish." To the computer, Goldwasser realised with a certain wistful pang, he himself, Nobbs, Nunn, and Chiddingfold, were all indifferently "Mr. Computer." So was the computer. Oil heaters and cigarette ends did not become circumstantially and wordily involved with shavings, waste paper, woodwork, or soft furnishings; fire horror struck. If fire horror struck twice in the same town within the year, They Are Calling It Doom Town. If the fire went on for longer than usual it was a fire marathon; if it was a small fire it was a mini-blaze; if it was in Russia it was a fireski. The world was also full of Mystery Men. Though there was never any mystery about who was behind a crime. It was a Master Mind, which was perhaps why the crime wave was, unlike most of the other waves which Britannia ruled, a permanent one.

Large sections of the English language were also rendered otiose by replacing long words with small words hyphenated together. Unilateralists were ban-the-bomb marchers. Save-the-horses men had a beat-the-rush plan for dodge-the-ban traders. No-overtime men met oh-so-friendly call-off-the-strike officials for let's-be-sensible talks. On-off-on-off plans for get-you-home services started who-is-to-blame storms.

Newspaper language, in fact, was a simplification to the point of abstraction. It was like mathematics. It had a bearing on life, but was remote from it, making not particular statements but general ones. Just as $2+2=4$ applies to any two pairs of apples, or vacuum-cleaners, or middle-class Frenchmen, so "Mr. Average in Get-There-Or-Else Mystery Marathon" described a range of situations so undefined as to be infinite. The more Goldwasser thought about it, the more difficult it was to see what sort of evidence could possibly disprove "Mr. Average in Get-There-or-Else Mystery Marathon," and if there was no evidence that disproved it, there was plainly none that proved it, either. The only possible conclusion was that it was not a factual statement at all, but, like $2+2=4$, a well-formed formula legitimately derived from an axiomatic system. All this was a great comfort to Goldwasser, who had to reproduce the system on the axiomatic machinery of a computer.

Bearing all this in mind, he had set up enough cards in the card-index to begin processing simple stories along these lines. The results were not perfect, but they had a certain encouraging purity of style—particularly the Magic, or Black, Box One, which according to analysis of cuttings, normally appeared about once a fortnight. There were several different permutations, but they all looked more or less like:

"MAGIC BOX" WILL HELP HOUSEWIVES
TOP SECRET BRITISH TRIUMPH

British scientists have developed a "magic box," it was learned last night. The new wonder device was tested behind locked doors after years of research.

Results were said to have surpassed expectations.

Top brass were among the men in the mystery research marathon. Last night experts were calling the magic box the beat-the-jinx box. The new wonder device has broken the jinx that has haunted British wonder projects ever since last week.

97

Mrs. Average Housewife will be among the first to feel the benefit of the beat-the-jinx box.

How does it work?

Specially designed tubes feed supplies of wonder drug into the mechanism. A magic eye keeps a continuous check.

The device is switched on and off with a switch which works on the same principle as an ordinary domestic light switch.

A secret ray device is activated by an activator.

But the real secret of the magic box?—A new all-British wonder cell.

Goldwasser had arranged the cards so that the results they produced showed the two conflicting tropisms of newspaper language—on the one hand towards a range of especially familiar expressions like "do-it-yourself," "scorcher," "hubby," and "television," and on the other hand towards an exotic range of words that never occurred anywhere else, like "envoy," "slay," "blaze," and "pinpoint." The stories that emerged had something of the poignant ambiguity of the pictures one sees in the clouds—glimpses of a remote, fantastic world at once familiar and yet chimeric. For instance:

DO-IT-YOURSELF ENVOY IN SOCCER PROBE MARATHON
Rain horror ended Britain's miracle heatwave last night. Millions of viewers saw the man they call Mr. X, the mystery man in the Sex-in-the-Snow case, mention the Royal Family on TV.

Mr. X—a Mayfair playboy well-known in Café Society and the International Set—will pinpoint the area where shapely brunette "Mrs. Undies" says her wonder hubby sent her to Coventry.

Police with tracker dogs and firemen with breathing apparatus fought to bring the mini-miracle under control.

Thirty-two year-old hole-in-the-head secrets man "Mr. Showbiz" collapsed after a Dolce-Vita-type milk stout orgy. In a plush night-club doctors struggled desperately to save his life.

But it overpowered them and escaped.

Top scientists threw a cordon round the doomed area. The trapped men retaliated by throwing a dragnet round the scientists, and going through them with a fine-tooth comb to locate the missing super-horror in a twelve-minute mini-marathon.

Later a mini-man assisted the police in their inquiries.

After a certain initial prejudice against this sort of language had dissolved, Goldwasser began to enjoy the stories his programme wrote. They seemed to him to be the real modern fairy stories, and the cloudy, ambiguous world they revealed of miracle hubby horrors he came to see as the true fairyland lurking just round the corner of every Englishman's consciousness. To a remarkable degree, moreover, the stories survived his compulsion to read them backwards with their sense unimpaired.

21

Nunn's work was being seriously affected. His raw squash production was down by twenty per cent. His rugby watching had fallen by twenty-five. His output of crude sporting conversation had slumped by nearly a third. If things got any worse, it occurred to him, he might have to get Miss Fram to take some of his sporting obligations off his shoulders in her spare time. If she had any spare time. He wondered anxiously whether she did, or whether she remained in the outer office all night as well as all day, faffling away at whatever it was she faffled away at. How little, reflected Nunn sadly, do we know about our fellow creatures when one comes down to it!

The trouble was Goldwasser. Nunn had got on to one or two of his old friends in security and told them about the Goldwasser case. They had been interested—"*Very* interested, Naismith" (as they called Nunn for security reasons)—and they had put a man on to watch Goldwasser.

The man had found out some rather interesting things about Goldwasser ("*Very* interesting things, Naismith!" as the men whom Nunn for security reasons called Jurgensen and Bissel had remarked, puffing at their pipes and wrinkling their foreheads significantly.) The difficulty was to make sense of it all, to fit all the pieces of the jig-saw together.

In the privacy of his office Nunn sorted through the reports yet again. At 1630 hours on Plumday, as Monday was called for security reasons, Goldwasser had consumed two cups of tea and a chocolate-coated wafer bar in the Tea Room. On Spoonday he had twice come out of his laboratory, scratched his head and gone back inside again. At 1143 hours on Troutday he had left the Institute and gone to J. Groombridge, Ironmonger, where he had stayed four minutes and purchased a dozen half-inch screws, brass, round-headed, which he had told the assistant he wanted in order to put up a mirror.

There were clearly any number of insecure things that could be done with the help of a chocolate-coated wafer bar, twelve brass screws, and a mirror. Already the possible explanations had proliferated to an extent which made critical assessment almost impossible. Then on Beanday Goldwasser had been to a cinema club to see Pudovkin's *Mother*, and then to an Odeon to see *Charlie's Aunt*, after which he had gone to an Indian restaurant and ordered a chicken biriani, a bhindi ghosht, and three poppadoms.

Nunn's mind reeled. Why had Goldwasser twice scratched his head in the same place? Who was Pudovkin's mother? Why three poppadoms, and not two, or four? There were rational answers to these questions. There was, somewhere, a pattern in which twelve brass screws, two head scratchings, and three poppadoms had their place. There had to be a pattern. The whole possibility of intelligence work depended upon there being a definite natural order in the universe, a discoverable pattern behind the reports which the Jurgensens and Bissels submitted.

The most suggestive report was one dated Teaday, which recorded that at 1300 hours precisely Goldwasser had emerged from his laboratory, stopped in the corridor to scratch his head, and then left the building, to return ten minutes later carrying a picnic lunch which he had consumed at his desk.

Why should Goldwasser stop so deliberately to scratch his head? Normally a man wishing to scratch his head in those circumstances would do it in private, before leaving his room, or if caught short by an urgent desire to scratch it as he walked along the corridor, would try to do it inconspicuously as he went along. And why had Goldwasser eaten a "picnic lunch?" And why at 1300 hours? Because, good God, wasn't 1300 hours one o'clock in the morning? Nunn had never been able to remember which way round the twenty-four hour clock was. But he was pretty damned sure 1300 hours was 1 a.m.! In fact he was absolutely certain it was! A so-called picnic lunch consumed at dead of night! This was certainly something to get one's teeth into! What in the name of heaven could it mean?

Nunn stared at the report, his brain overwhelmed by the immensity of the information it was going to yield up to him. He pulled his Compleat Angler's Diary towards him and wrote on it in large letters:

MIDNIGHT LUNCH

He underlined it. Then he wrote underneath in slightly smaller letters:

Ironmonger—3 poppadoms

Then he tore the page out and burned it in the ash-tray for security reasons.

On a fresh page he began to construct a graph showing the daily frequency of Goldwasser's head-scratching against his consumption of chocolate wafers in the Tea Room, marking on the line the Ironmonger and Midnight Lunch incidents under the code-names SEAHORSE and OVERMANTEL.

He stared at it until it blurred before his eyes. Perhaps he had confused the code-words, and Beanday was Monday and Spoonday was Friday. Or was Troutday Monday, and Plumday Tuesday, and Spoonday Thursday? Or had he just forgotten the days of the week? How the devil did they go? Sunday, Plumday, Tuesday, Spoonday ... ? Plumday, Monday, Spoonday, Bensday ... ? *Bensday*? What was this nonsense? *Wumsday*, for heaven's sake.

Suddenly he had a great moment of insight. Goldwasser had bought twelve brass screws in the IRONMONGERS to fix the OVERMANTEL!

A second flash of understanding followed almost immediately. Goldwasser had bought the three POPPADOMS for the MIDNIGHT LUNCH—one for himself, one for writing messages on, and one for the SEAHORSE!

It all tied up. A pattern was beginning to emerge. He was starting to make sense of what at first had appeared to be some of the most puzzling data to come his way in his whole career in intelligence.

He looked at the reports again, and at once another question struck him—a question which might just possibly be the key to the whole mystery. He pulled out his Amateur Wrestler and Judo World Diary, and noted in the space marked Memo:

"Ask 'Bissel' and 'Jurgensen' who 'Naismith'."

He put the diary back in his pocket, and tottered agedly out to find someone to play a game of bowls with.

22

Rowe had started his novel once again. Chapter 1 (he wrote). *No Particle Forgot.*

There was a cry from the terrace. Shielding his eyes against the hard, almost tangible glare of the noonday Mediterranean sun, Rick looked up.

Rick Roe was tall. But his shoulders were broad, so that the first impression you got of him was that he was a man of average build standing some way off. Some might have called him handsome, but Rick did not think of himself as being so. His features were almost classically even, but the mouth had a certain humorous twist which made the statuesque proportions of the face seem gratefully human. The mouth, in fact, was interesting. The regular teeth stood out very white amid his deep tan, while the lips were firm but somehow sensuous, belying the almost ascetic nose. The eyes were blue—like aquamarines nestling among the jeweller's crumpled chamois leather as he narrowed his gaze against the hard, almost tangible noonday glare. The eyebrows were russet thickets—slightly raised, as if surprised and perhaps a little scandalised to find themselves sitting on top of a pair of aquamarines. The hair was russet, too—cut *en brosse*, and there were fine russet hairs gleaming along the forearm raised to ward off the hard, almost tangible noonday glare.

He was wearing a faded blue shirt, which looked as if it had been splashed and soaked in salt water a great deal. The shirt was tucked into a pair of whitish canvas trousers, held up by a narrow leather belt. The buckle on the belt was simple—a plain loop of brass of the sort that could be seen fastening the belt that held up the stained trousers of a thousand sunburnt men lounging or strolling on the quays of any Mediterranean port.

But it was the shoes that held the attention. They were cheap espadrilles made of worn blue canvas. The laces had once been white, but were white no more, and the lace in the right shoe was a deeper shade of grey than its fellow in the left. The soles of the shoes were made of coiled rope, and one imagined, without quite knowing why, that they would have black stains of tar on the bottom of them.

Rick could feel the roughness of his fingers against his deeply sunburnt brow as he gazed. His fingers were long— surprisingly long and fine for such a well-built man. The nails were cut square, and shone like the mother-of-pearl Rick saw when he was skin-diving off the end of the island.

The fingers grew from strong, well-formed hands, with russet hair on the back of them, and the hands were attached to the muscular arms by broad, sinewy wrists. There were four fingers and a thumb on each hand . . .

Rowe stopped. There was a great deal more to be said before Rick could be taken as fully established, of course—the number of buttons on his shirt, the thickness of the hair on his chest, the size of his shoes, whether his trousers were done up with buttons or a zip. But perhaps it would be best to skip it for now and go on with the next bit before he lost the thread of the narrative.

The cry had come from the terrace, and it was at this that Rick was now gazing.

The terrace was an area of paving, studded with shrubs and ornamental urns, covering about half an acre of land. It was at the top of a bluff, covered with parched grass, loose rocks, stunted bougainvillæa and fuchsia bushes, that fell fairly sharply down to the beach. On the lower slopes of the bluff a few wild flowers struggled with the aridity of the sub-soil for a meagre existence. The only other spots of colour in the scene were a few tin cans and pieces of orange peel scattered among the grey of the pebbles and the dark green, almost black, of sun-dried seaweed.

A path led upwards from the beach, zig-zagging among the bougainvillæa, now disappearing behind a rock, now reappearing to cross a stretch of open ground. The path lay in the bottom of a sort of broad gulley that climbed the bluff between two vertical ribs of rock—gigantic buttresses that looked from a distance like splashes of umber paint down the cliff-face, but were, in fact, gigantic buttresses. The whole scene was a lunar landscape of jutting rocks, tumbled stones, and parching soil—splashed everywhere one looked, of course, with bougainvillæa.

The importance of the bluff was clear; it held up the terrace from which the cry had come . . .

Rowe stopped again. Heavens, he had scarcely started to describe the scene. He had not explained what you could see in the distance. He had not said whether the sea was blue. He had not even established which month it was, or whether the bluff faced east, west, north, or south. He had not yet brought in the great storehouse of zinnias, azaleas, robinsonia, forsythia, flowering pangloss, jacantha, orodigia, smithia, old lady's bedsock, putria, and Peloponnesian daisies he had up his sleeve yet. Never mind. He could come back and plant those later at his leisure. The important thing now was to keep the excitement of the story going.

. . . the whole scene shimmering in the hard, almost tangible noonday glare.

That cry again. Gazing upwards, Rick saw that it had come from a girl who was standing on the terrace. It was Nina Pleschkov. Even across the quarter mile or so that separated them Rick could see that she was beautiful. She was slim, with high, pointed breasts. Her tawny hair fell about her sunburnt shoulders. Her lips seemed somehow very red in that glaring white light, and the eyes that moved almost humorously beneath the delicate, dark eyebrows were green.

She had a delicately carved chin, with a nose that promised its owner had a mind of her own, and high, pointed cheeks. The boyishness of her slim thighs was set off by the very feminine promise of the shirt casually but deeply open at her neck.

Her ears were small, but firm. Her elbows, coming at the mid-point of her arms, looked almost like a young boy's . . .

Again Rowe stopped. Navel, knees, calves, toes, thumbs, shoulder-blades—still all undescribed! Not to mention her clothes. Not a word yet of her height, or of any identifying marks! Was he interested in her as a woman or not? If he didn't get it all down, wouldn't every reader in the land immediately leap to the conclusion that she had knobbly knees, or three thumbs, or a deformed navel? Never mind. Get on for now to the next bit of action—and that, allowing for the material still to be put in, would bring him right through to the last few lines of the first chapter.

He fetched himself a cup of tea, and then wrote them:

Again the cry rang out from the terrace. In that clear, still air, every syllable was plainly audible where Rick stood. Indeed, they had been perfectly audible the first time, but one could not react too quickly when there was so much to be explained, so much described.

"Lunch-time!" cried Nina.

And still the hard, almost tangible noonday glare beat down.

23

"Yes," said Rowe, but on reflection that sounded a shade facile, and he rephrased it. "Y-e-e-e-e-s," he said.

"I mean," said Macintosh, "there are plenty of other people in the Institute who've got their eye on the new wing. Oh, yes. I'm told there's a group—no names, no pack drill—who want to hold some sort of huge sexual orgy in there."

"Yes, so I hear."

"They'll never get away with it, of course. I'm told Nunn's furious about it. It makes you think, though. I mean, the things I could use that wing for if only I had the time! If only I could get away from my damned Samaritans for a week or two! Did I ever tell you about my idea for programming a computer to write pornographic novels? Well, I sometimes wonder if you couldn't programme machines to perform a great deal of human sexual behaviour. It would save a lot of labour."

"Yes," said Rowe. "Yes."

"At any rate in the early stages. On the same principle you might also programme machines to go through the initial conversational moves two people make when they first meet. They're always standardised, like chess openings. You could select your gambit, then go away and make the tea while the machine played it, and come back and pick up the conversation when it started to become interesting."

"Yes," said Rowe.

"It breaks my heart to see that wing going empty when there's so much to be done. I mean, let's accept—and I owe this suggestion to my good friend Goldwasser—that all ethical systems are ossified, in which case all operations within an ethical system can be performed by computer. I should be designing circuits to demonstrate what happens when one ossified sys-

tem, say a Christian one, comes into contact with another ossified system, say a liberal agnostic one. And what happens when
two computers with incompatible systems try to programme a
third between them.

"Ah, Rowe, Rowe, Rowe! Doesn't it move you to contem-
plate the great areas of life which have ossified, where activity
has been reduced to the manipulation of a finite range of variables? The pity and the terror of it, Rowe! These vast petrified
forests are our rightful domain. They are waiting helplessly to
be brought under the efficient, benevolent rule of the kindly
computer.

"Take the field of religious devotions. What computer man
can survey devotional practice without lifting up his heart and
thanking God for sending him such a prize? When we are called
in to write a programme for automated devotion—as we shall
be in five or ten years' time—we shall of course recommend per-
forming all the religious services in the country from one central computer, which would also write its own sermons,
logically developing any given topic along the lines laid down
by the Thirty-Nine Articles or the Holy Office without fear of
heterodoxy. But in fifteen or twenty years' time we shall be writing programmes for praying. The subjects and sentiments tend
to come in a fairly limited range."

"Ah," said Rowe, "there's a difference between a man and a
machine when it comes to praying."

"Aye. The machine would do it better. It wouldn't pray for
things it oughtn't to pray for, and its thoughts wouldn't wan-
der."

"Y-e-e-s. But the computer saying the words wouldn't be the
same . . ."

"Oh, I don't know. If the words 'O Lord, bless the Queen and
her Ministers' are going to produce any tangible effects on the
Government it can't matter who or what says them, can it?"

"Y-e-e-s, I see that. But if a man says the words he *means*
them."

"So does the computer. Or at any rate, it would take a

damned complicated computer to say the words *without* meaning them. I mean, what do we mean by 'mean'? If we want to know whether a man or a computer *means* 'O Lord, bless the Queen and her Ministers,' we look to see whether it's grinning insincerely or ironically as it says the words. We try to find out whether it belongs to the Communist Party. We observe whether it simultaneously passes notes about lunch or fornication. If it passes all the tests of this sort, what other tests *are* there for telling if it means what it says? All the computers in my department, at any rate, would pray with great sincerity and single-mindedness. They're devout wee things, computers."

"Y-e-e-e-s. But I take it you don't believe in a God who hears and answers prayers?"

"That's not my end of the business. I'm just concerned with getting the praying done with maximum efficiency and minimum labour output."

"But, Macintosh, if you're as cynical as that, what do you think the difference between man and computer is?"

"I'm not absolutely certain, Rowe. I'm inclined to rule out what you might call 'soul.' I should think that in time we could teach computer to be overwhelmed by the sound of Bach or the sight of another computer, to distinguish between good sonnets and bad, and to utter uplifting sentiments at the sight of the Matterhorn or the sunset. Obviously it's not the faculty of choice; computer can be programmed to choose, just as man does, rationally, anti-rationally, at random, or by any combination of the three. Some people, of course, have set a certain store by the human capacity for faith. But I don't think it helps us much here. If you tell computer that the sky is green, computer will believe you. Or you could programme computer to perceive empirically that the sky is blue, but to act on a profound, unspoken faith that it is green. Think of that, Rowe! And if you objected that this faith was forced on him willy-nilly, then you might imagine a computer programmed to choose whether to believe the evidence of his senses that the sky is blue, or whether in spite of what he saw to accept that it was green because its operator had told him it was."

"I suppose so," said Rowe.

"Now you and I, Rowe, as practical men, would say that the only useful working distinction between man and computer is that computer can choose only from among a finite range of variables, whereas man can specify for himself the range of variables from which he will choose. But it's a wee bit tenuous, because it depends simply on the complexity of man's neuro-mechanism. I suppose one day we shall build a computer as complex, and it will begin to specify its own limitations."

"Of course," said Rowe.

"I dare say, in the long run, the distinction will prove to be an economic one, you know. In the same way that it's cheaper to use a computer for finite intellectual tasks, there may well come a point beyond which the open-endedness of a once-only job would require a computer so complex and so specialised that it would be cheaper to use a human being. Aye, I believe there will always remain certain areas on the fringes of the petrified forest where original thoughts have to be thought, and original juxta-positions of ideas made, and new meanings and possibilities seen. I shouldn't be surprised if it proved more economical to use men rather than man-like computers to work these areas. As a computer man I naturally regret it. But as a human being I must admit I get a certain sneaking pleasure from believing that there are jobs to be done which are worthy of the human mind. The awe and terror of it, Rowe! The pity and the grandeur! Do you see what I mean?"

"Yes," said Rowe, as they got up from their table in the Tea Room to return to their laboratories. "Yes. Yes."

He felt slightly exhausted, but also exhilarated. What a stu-pendous countryside of propositions they had marched through! Petrified forests! Infinite ranges of variables! Computers really deeply religious things! Sincerity! Choice! Complexity! Man all right after all! He felt a great sense of com-radeship with Macintosh, who had borne him company on this extraordinary journey. An extract from a review hung in lights in the sky above the infinite forests and the petrified ranges, and he felt both generously pleased—and moved that he was generously pleased—to see that for once the celestial reviewer referred not to him but to Macintosh. "Macintosh ..." it said "... A wonderful listener ... brings out all the dazzling intellectual curiosity in Rowe ..."

24

Sir Prestwick Wining was on the line for Nunn. The fact was well-established.

"Sir Prestwick Wining for you, Mr. Nunn," said Miss Fram in the outer office.

"Mr. Nunn?" said Sir Prestwick's secretary. "Sir Prestwick Wining for you, Mr. Nunn."

"Nunn?" demanded Sir Prestwick anxiously. "Nunn? Is that you, Nunn?"

"Good morning, Sir Prestwick," said Nunn.

"Is that Nunn speaking?"

"Right here, Sir Prestwick."

"Ah. Well, look, this is Wining here."

"Hallo, Sir Prestwick."

"Good morning, Nunn."

There was a pause, while both men recovered from the strain of negotiations so far and tried to remember which of them it was who was phoning the other, and what about. The silence might have fooled someone who did not know how these matters are negotiated. At any rate, it fooled the switchboard girl at Amalgamated Television, and she pulled the plug out.

Nunn's telephone rang again in about five minutes' time.

"Sir Prestwick Wining for you, Mr. Nunn," said Miss Fram.

"Sir Prestwick Wining for you, Mr. Nunn," said Sir Prestwick's secretary.

"Nunn?" interrogated Sir Prestwick keenly. "Nunn? Nunn? Is that Nunn? Am I through? Nunn? Nunn?"

"Speaking, Sir Prestwick."

"It's Wining again, Nunn. Nunn, what happened? Something happened. I couldn't hear you. Were we cut off?"

"We must have been."

"Look, Nunn, could you hear me?"

"Not a word, Sir Prestwick."

"Then you missed what I said about Rothermere being extremely upset?"

"Yes."

"You heard it?"

"No, I missed it."

"Well, look, I'll say it again. Rothermere is extremely upset."

"I'm sorry to hear that."

"Yes. Well, he's upset about the possible repercussions, you see. As I explained before—perhaps you didn't hear—it's not that he wants to interfere in any way with the Institute's traditional academic freedom. He believes—and of course I fully agree—that it should be completely inviolable. Completely."

"I appreciate that feeling, Sir Prestwick."

"But there are the possible repercussions to be considered. Do you see what I mean?"

"Oh, entirely."

"I've made myself clear?"

"Oh, absolutely, Sir Prestwick."

"We understand one another, then?"

"I think we do."

"No hard feelings?"

"Far from it."

"A nod's as good as a wink, eh, Nunn?"

"Any day, Sir Prestwick."

"Well, that's settled, then. I hope I didn't sound too stuffed shirt about it, Nunn. You know how it is. Rothermere's been very up in the air. Blames me for not finding out and letting him know, which puts me in rather a spot. He says he can't think what object there is in my being on the board if he still has to find out how his money's being spent by listening to the gossip at parties. I can see his point, of course."

"Listening to the gossip at parties?"

"Yes, he heard all about the present stink at some party he went to. I told you about it. Or did you miss that bit, too?"

"I must have done."

"Well, some B.B.C. woman told him about it at a party. That's how he found out. It was particularly aggravating that someone in the B.B.C. knew more about Amalgamated's affairs than he did."

"I see."

"So of course he was furious."

"Of course he was."

"Justifiably, I think."

"Oh, entirely."

"It's just the repercussions we're thinking of, Nunn."

"Exactly."

"I mean, it's not that we personally think there's anything wrong in having computers that conduct religious services . . ."

"Computers that conduct religious services?"

"Didn't you hear anything I said before, Nunn?"

"I certainly didn't hear anything about computers conducting religious services."

"Well, that's what Rothermere's so upset about. Your people are apparently planning to fix up these computers in the new Ethics Wing."

"Are they?"

"Well, according to this woman in the B.B.C. She said you were going to have computers praying down there . . ."

"*Praying? Computers praying*? Whatever will these scientist chappies think of next?"

"She said you were going to have computers celebrating communion and hearing confessions."

"Really? Well, I'll get on to this at once, Sir Prestwick."

"I mean, it's just the repercussions we're worried about."

"I'll jump on it, Sir Prestwick. Trust me."

"You have to be terribly careful about things like repercussions in our industry."

"Of course you do."

"I suppose this is your man Macintosh up to his tricks again. Not a sound man, Macintosh, if I may venture to comment."

"I think you're wrong there, Sir Prestwick. He's pretty sound, is Macintosh."

"Sound, is he?"

"Pretty sound."

"Yes, well, I must say, he seems sound enough."

"Between ourselves, Sir Prestwick, I've a shrewd suspicion that the culprit will turn out to be Goldwasser."

"Goldwasser, eh?"

"I'm afraid he's a born troublemaker."

"Well, I must admit I've never liked him myself. There's something about him that rather puts one off."

"Not a nice man, I'm afraid."

"Not a nice man at all."

"Don't you worry, Sir Prestwick. I'll take Mr. Goldwasser's number."

"Fair enough. Did you hear me say my compliments to your good lady before?"

"I didn't, as a matter of fact."

"Well, then, my compliments to your good lady."

25

"This is Mr. Goldwasser, Your Majesty," said Riddle, as Nobbs shook hands with Haugh.

"No, no, no," smiled Mrs. Plushkov with exasperating patience. "That's not Goldwasser, Riddle. That's Riddle."

"For crying out loud," snarled Riddle. "He *can't* be. Goldwasser's Riddle."

"But my dear Riddle, you forget that Riddle is Plushkov."

Everyone was standing in the lobby, glaring at each other, or leaning hopelessly against the walls and staring dully at the floor. The whole staff of the Institute was tired and cross. They had been in the corridors all week, rehearsing for the Official Opening, and they all had that dreary, crushed feeling in their intestines that comes from standing around for a long time without knowing exactly what one is supposed to be doing.

What they were trying to do was to time the various sections of the visit against a stop-watch, since the Co-ordinating Committee was advised by the Sub-Committee on Timing that these occasions always had to be rehearsed down to the last second. But it was not easy. The "Balmoral" scissors, the jewelled switch, the gas-fired golden taper, and all the rest of the equipment had not yet arrived from the Empire Ceremonial Supply Company, and there was still no apparatus of any sort in the new wing itself. The missing links were replaced by a variety of more or less unsatisfactory substitutes and hypotheses, as were all the official guests whose hands would have to be shaken on the day, and one or two of the senior staff, like Nunn and Macintosh, who were impressive enough not to be argued with when they said they were too busy to attend. So, for the sake of rehearsals, Rowe was Vulgurian, Riddle was Nunn, and Goldwasser was Macintosh, which meant that Plushkov had to be Riddle and Haugh Goldwasser. No, Riddle had to be Goldwasser, and . . . or was it Rowe who was Goldwasser?

The only point on which everyone was clear was that the principal deficiency, the Queen herself, was being supplied by Nobbs. He was not an ideal surrogate sovereign, or even a willing one, but when the Joint Committee for Understudying had appealed to Heads of Departments to spare someone for the job, Goldwasser had spared Nobbs before anyone else could think.

Now Goldwasser was regretting his generosity. It was bad enough to have Nobbs about the laboratory all day, humping his resentful bag of ill-articulated bones back and forth, catching the corners of desks with his thighs and knocking them slightly out of line. But to spend his days shaking Nobbs's limp hand over and over again, and calling him "Ma'am," was less agreeable still. As the rehearsals wore on, Goldwasser became increasingly concerned about the hand's remarkable limpness. So far as Goldwasser could tell, it was not exactly a natural limpness. Nobbs kept his hand limp when he shook hands because he had read that the firm grasp he had affected as an adolescent to create the impression of a strong character was merely an affectation designed to create the impression of a strong character. But then Nobbs wore a beard because he had read that since it was generally believed that only men with weak chins wore beards, no one with a weak chin would wear a beard for fear of being thought to have a weak chin; therefore, it could be deduced that anyone who wore a beard had in fact a strong chin; and in this way Nobbs grew a beard to hide his weak chin. Or so Goldwasser believed. Altogether there was something about Nobbs that was two-faced—or not so much two-faced as three-faced, with one face watching the other two.

"Let's go right back to the beginning," said Mrs. Plushkov. "Opening positions, please, everyone."

There was a weary groan. Goldwasser felt his crushed intestines pack down a little farther.

"Jellicoe," said Mrs. Plushkov to the janitor as they all trooped outside into the forecourt, "don't slam the car door this time until Nobbs is well clear of it. Remember, you've got seven seconds before she—he—Nobbs is supposed to be on his feet on the pavement. Now, is One ready? Let's take it from—*now*."

Jellicoe stepped forward and opened an imaginary car door. Nobbs lurched out of the imaginary car.

"Steady, Nobbs," said Mrs. Plushkov.

"Good afternoon," said Chiddingfold, and led Nobbs across to the guard of honour of laboratory technicians.

"Stop!" cried Mrs. Plushkov.

There was a general sigh. Jellicoe took out a pocket mirror and began to examine his moustache. Nobbs sat down on the edge of the pavement. Goldwasser tried to shuffle part of his weight on to a narrow ornamental ledge. He knew what the delay was. The Conversation Committee had gone into emergency session yet again. They would be discussing whether Chiddingfold should be asked to elaborate his greeting with a few conversational remarks. There was a faction which favoured the Director's making some comment on the weather. There was another faction which felt that any comment on the weather would present difficulties in timing; since the exact text could not be decided upon until the day, and that some remark about the royal car would be preferable. "How many miles to the gallon do you get out of her, ma'am?" was thought to be the most generally acceptable. But finally the committee would face up to the impossibility of putting any of this to Chiddingfold, and would vote to postpone a decision until the next meeting. Goldwasser gazed hopelessly at a patch of ground about one foot square just in front of his shoes.

"Let's go on again, please," cried Mrs. Plushkov. "From where we stopped."

Nobbs shambled across to the guard of honour of laboratory technicians.

"For inspection," shouted the Senior Laboratory Technician, "port—slide rules!"

"Up, two, three," called Mrs. Plushkov. "In, two, three. Ragged, very ragged."

Nobbs barged along the ranks, treading on the right marker's toe, and knocking another man's slide rule out of his hands.

"Steady, Nobbs," said Mrs. Plushkov.

"Ease—cursors!" shouted the Senior Laboratory Technician.

"Three seconds under," said Mrs. Plushkov. "You were cutting the corners, Nobbs."

Nobbs lumbered across to the foot of the steps, received a bouquet from Chiddingfold's small daughter, deputised for by Miss Fram, and reeled on into the lobby to meet the assembled staff and guests.

"Stop!" cried Mrs. Plushkov. "Nomenclature Committee around me, please!"

Goldwasser subsided weakly against a wall. The Nomenclature Committee was his fault. In a light-hearted moment one day he had suggested that calling Nobbs "Your Majesty" might strictly speaking constitute an act of sedition, and within two days the question was being urgently debated throughout the thirty-seven committees. Almost everyone agreed that a seditious interpretation could be put upon the usage, and that to continue using it might open the Institute to the possibility of prosecution or blackmail. But the practical problem was what to call Nobbs if not Her Majesty. It would be ridiculous, everyone said, to expect people to bow and curtsy to him and call him Nobbs. The original smile had scarcely faded from Goldwasser's face before the Nomenclature Committee had been set up, to compose a formula which would both command respect and correspond more closely to the realities of Nobbs's situation. Various working parties and study groups had so far produced:

> Your Humility
> Your Servitude
> Your Ordinariness
> Your Humanity
> Your Anonymity
> Your Proxyship
> Your Beardedness

Your Nobbs
Your Principal Research Assistantship

Once more, Goldwasser knew, the decision would have to be postponed.

"Carry on from where we were," shouted Mrs. Plushkov. "Go on calling Nobbs 'Your Majesty' for to-day. Let me once again ask everyone to use his discretion, and not to talk about this outside the Institute."

Hands were shaken, at five seconds per hand, then off went everyone on the tour of the establishment, at two feet per second. Into a department. Meet typical Research Assistant (Grade One) and look at typical computer (12 seconds). Ask typical question about computer (say, 5 seconds). Get typical answer (15 seconds). Express appreciation of work done (say, 4 seconds).

On down corridor, at two feet per second, up stairs at two seconds per stair, and into next department. Meet typical Research Assistant (Grade Two) and ask typical personal question (say, 10 seconds). Get typically modest answer (1 second). Comment on pleasantness of view out of window (say, 5 seconds). Deputy-Director explains how fortunate Institute is in this respect (31 seconds). Adds polite joke (3 seconds). Laughter (26 seconds). Public amazement at how informal and charming Nobbs is (4 seconds). Out, striking ill-articulated Nobbs thigh against table and bringing down three files, a bottle of ink, and 140 loose sheets of foolscap manuscript. Recriminations all round (20 minutes).

For Goldwasser the afternoon began to go by in a dream. It was interrupted momentarily when he was caught a sharp blow on the side of the head with a window-pole which was being used as a substitute for the golden taper to light a flame of undying remembrance to those who fell in the Luddite riots. At another point he was conscious of a limp hand being thrust authoritatively into his, and a well-known voice saying "Wakey wakey, mate." And there were a few moments of wonderful sitting down when the Special Purposes Committee met to consider once again whether time should be allowed for Nobbs to powder his nose.

Then they were in the new wing, and Rowe, deputising for Macintosh, was showing Nobbs all the equipment so far installed, which consisted of several office tables and a number of chairs. Almost the last thing Goldwasser was conscious of was Rowe reading off a piece of paper:

"And this is a table, ma'am. What in essence it consists of is a horizontal rectilinear plane surface maintained by four vertical columnar supports, which we call legs. The tables in this laboratory, ma'am, are as advanced in design as one will find anywhere in the world."

Which was how, when everybody else was standing up for the National Anthem, Goldwasser came to be lying on the floor, sprawling face downwards with great casualness. Nunn, who was keeping an eye on various security aspects from a discreet distance, was not surprised. The case against Goldwasser was open and closed already; he would be in no position to demonstrate his feelings about the National Anthem on the day.

What Nunn was really worrying about now was Nobbs's thighs. The more he saw of them in action the less he liked them. Were they a secret weapon in the pay of Goldwasser? They didn't appear to be in the pay of Nobbs. He watched them intently as they knocked things off desks and split chairs they came up against. They appeared to pursue their programme of sabotage and disruption quite independently of Nobbs.

Of course, they might be *unconscious* agents of Goldwasser's. It was possible that Nobbs had been brainwashed by Goldwasser without knowing about it. But then so might anyone else in the room. Such things could happen. Nobody who was in security was likely to underestimate what could be done these days with brainwashing techniques. For all Nunn knew, he might have been brainwashed himself. He might well be an unconscious agent of Goldwasser's. His whole campaign against Goldwasser might be the result of a post-hypnotic suggestion implanted by Goldwasser himself. Indeed, his very realisation that he might be acting under Goldwasser's orders, even as Goldwasser took his ease down there on the floor, might itself be a response engineered by Goldwasser.

As soon as the anthem was over he retired to his room and brooded for a long time over a favourite niblick. These were deep waters he was fishing, and in deep waters there was nothing to do but keep one's eye on the ball and wait for an opening. He took a nap to clear his head and was awakened, greatly refreshed, by the sound of the Director collapsing heavily into his chair in the office next door after finishing the day's rehearsals. The Director, when he went in to see him, looked surprisingly old and tired, and Nunn spent nearly an hour trying to cheer him up by telling him the full medical histories of everyone who had dropped dead while running the marathon.

26

In the end Macintosh tacitly admitted that the ethical behaviour pattern of Samaritan II, which refused to throw itself overboard to save a sandbag, and so took the sandbag to the bottom with it as well, was unsatisfactory. He developed Samaritan III, which not only refused to sacrifice itself for an organism simpler than itself, but kept the raft afloat by pushing the simpler organism overboard.

"Look at it, man," he cried to Goldwasser, awed by his own handiwork, as they watched Samaritan III ruthlessly toss first a sandbag and then a sheep over the side. "That's a terrible sight, Goldwasser, a great and terrible sight. All the pity and the grandeur of man's struggle for survival are there. And yet this same Samaritan III when faced by Man, in the person of Sinson, does not hesitate to cast itself away. Perhaps we have an analogy here with the human mind's intuition of the divine. What we have beyond any doubt is a skeletal yet fundamentally accurate model of behaviour that is both ethical and effective."

Goldwasser sighed. If there was one thing he found less congenial than believing himself stupider than Macintosh it was finding himself cleverer.

"Try putting two Samaritan IIIs on the raft together," he suggested gloomily.

Macintosh put two Samaritan IIIs on the raft together, and the result drove him back on to the defensive. At first he tried to claim that it was entirely in accordance with good sense and natural justice that both Samaritan Ills should throw themselves overboard.

"There is a certain nobility about their choosing to perish together which recalls the high ethic of romantic tragedy. I was thinking of Romeo and Juliet."

Goldwasser rubbed his chin nervously, and looked anywhere but at Macintosh, in a way that powerfully undermined Macintosh's arguments. Macintosh made a minor adjustment to the Samaritans, with the result that instead of throwing themselves overboard, they threw one another. He invited Goldwasser in to watch as the two ethical machines seized one another in a powerful lock and hurled one another into the water.

"Aye," said Macintosh, "we see before us all the pity and the terror of the human condition, whose inexorable logic requires men to struggle with their peers for life even to the point of mutual extinction."

"It sounds like the First World War," said Goldwasser.

"Exactly."

"Or an ape trap."

"An ape trap?"

"A bottle with a banana in it. The ape puts his hand in and seizes the banana, which makes his fist too big to get out of the bottle. Compelled by the inexorable necessity of the simian condition to hold on to the food, the ape remains attached to the bottle and dies of starvation."

Macintosh allowed himself to be piqued by this comparison. He let himself be piqued from time to time when he considered that Goldwasser had passed a certain reasonable bound of destructiveness in his criticism, in the belief that an occasional dose of pique was good for Goldwasser. He stopped speaking to him, and passed into the usual channels an anonymous minute appointing Goldwasser the chairman of a committee to install experiments in the new wing.

The information passed back and forth about the administrative machine, and it was some time before it reached Goldwasser himself. As soon as he heard, he hurried across to Macintosh's laboratory to tell him about it.

The noise in the Ethics Department was worse than ever. Goldwasser could hear it, like a football crowd trapped inside a bathroom, even as he was crossing the courtyard. When he got inside the door he saw why. The sides of the test tank were crowded with shouting spectators. Not only the staff of the department, but the Institute's gardener, some of the cleaning women, and a great number of secretaries and lab. boys from other departments. As Goldwasser struggled to find a way through them, to see what they were shouting about, it occurred to him that a considerable number of the people who were elbowing him back with such impersonal rudeness had no connection with the Institute at all.

"What's all this?" he asked a young man called Gaunt, a junior technician from his own department.

"Oh, hallo," said Gaunt. "It's the Samaritan IVs."

"Get in there, boy!" shouted a weatherbeaten little man just in front of Goldwasser. "Hurt him, boy! What are you waiting for, lad?"

"Walk over him!" roared another man, wearing an unbuttoned grey trench-coat with the belt hanging down, just behind Goldwasser. "Tread on him! Stamp on him!"

By the time Goldwasser had edged through to a sight of the tank the crowd was silent. It seemed to be some sort of lull. In the water one of the test rafts bobbed up and down, with a machine labelled Samaritan IV aboard it.

Suddenly Goldwasser realised there was something in the water next to the raft, wallowing darkly. A pair of variometer dials rose briefly above the surface and gazed vacantly at the crowd for a moment. It was another Samaritan IV.

"What the devil ... ?" whispered Goldwasser to the weatherbeaten man.

"He's finished," said the man. "The referee ought to stop the fight."

But just at that moment, with a great silver plume of water, the Samaritan overboard hurled itself at the raft and seized its fellow by the base-plate. The crowd roared. The Samaritan on the raft began to belabour the other one about the dials. At each crash or clank the crowd shouted louder.

"Look at him!" bellowed the man in the trench-coat to Goldwasser. "Isn't he a lovely, scientific fighter?"

Somewhere a bell sounded, and a laboratory assistant leaned down from the gantry with a boathook and separated the two ethical machines. Other men in dinghies hauled them back to opposite corners of the tank and set to work on them with spanners and screw-drivers. A little battery acid was trickling out of one of them, Goldwasser noticed.

"Six to four on the boy in the blue corner!" shouted a man on the far side of the tank, marking up the odds on a blackboard. "Three to one against a knockout! Come on, now, gentlemen. Who are the sports?"

Goldwasser found Macintosh putting a couple of pounds on the favourite.

"It may seem a little irregular," he said, "the promoter betting on his own fight. But I think it's important, in an ethical conflict like this, to be committed. Do you see? Because I think what we have here is the essential ethical situation in all its pity and terror. I hope it meets the objections you made to the earlier systems?"

"Listen, Macintosh," said Goldwasser. "I've been appointed chairman of the Ethics Wing Utilisation Committee."

"Congratulations," said Macintosh.

"I mean, it's not my idea."

"A damned good appointment, all the same."

"Look, I don't want to tread on your toes."

"Oh, I welcome it, I assure you."

"You're certain?"

"Of course. As you know, I didn't want to do it myself."

"No. Well, I don't really want to do it either, of course. I mean, I'm busy enough as it is."

"Nevertheless, you probably have a certain duty, don't you, Goldwasser?"

"Do I?"

"I imagine if you introspect a little you'll find you have a sense of obligation of some sort."

The bell went for the next round. Goldwasser pushed his way gloomily back to the door, prising apart unknown shoulders, elbowing strange stomachs, treading heavily on a plimsolled foot.

"Jolly good," said the owner of the foot, chuckling bravely, and squeezing Goldwasser's elbow. It was Nunn, who had a sporting fiver on the machine in the red corner. He watched Goldwasser thoughtfully as he pushed on, wondering who could possibly have put him in charge of the politically sensitive Ethics Wing Utilisation Committee. In an organisational set-up as complicated as this one, of course, it seemed a profitless speculation. Surprising, really, that it wasn't Macintosh's responsibility to install the experiments in the new wing. After all, he was the Head of the Department. Didn't seem to be anything to do with him, though. Odd, that. Perhaps somebody was keeping it away from him because they had something on him. It was unlikely with someone as sound as Macintosh. Still, one never knew. In security no one could be trusted. One was completely on one's own.

After his fiver had definitely gone down the drain, Nunn withdrew to his office for prolonged meditation on the matter, surrounding himself with all his golf clubs, lacrosse sticks, punchballs, running spikes, and scrum caps as a sort of dam to protect himself from the gradual seepage of Goldwasser into every corner of the universe. He pulled them all closely about him, like bedclothes. He was a lone wolf, and he would lie low high up here in his eyrie until the iron was hot, and when the iron was hot, wham!—he would come out like a tiger and knock it for six. The hour would strike, and in that hour he would be terrible!

"Jolly good," he told the spoons and the drivers quietly.

27

Rowe had moved on to Chapter II, but to signify his abandonment of the outworn style in which Chapter I was drafted he had retitled the novel *The Skulls of Glass*.

When Rick and Nina joined the others (*he wrote*) on the terrace in the shade of the great jeroboam tree, there was plainly a certain tension in the air. Fiddlingchild, the immensely rich oil magnate who was their host, looked thunderous. His mistress, the dark, sinuously beautiful Anna Riedl, impatiently tapped the immense emerald on her finger against the side of her cocktail glass, as she watched Stavros Nunopolos, the Greek playboy, loll back in a basket chair and joke with a studied fatuousness that was more polished than usual.

Watching Nunopolos, Rick knew that he was almost certain that Anna felt a passionate contempt for Fiddlingchild's failure to understand his, Nunopolos's, motives. Anna plainly knew that Nunopolos understood her feelings about Fiddlingchild, and she knew too that Nina knew she knew about Nunopolos's knowledge—and that if Nina knew, one must assume that Fiddlingchild could guess from the meaningful glance Nina shot at Rick that Nunopolos had divined emotions in Anna which could only relate to some failure of understanding in himself vis-à-vis Nunopolos.

All this Rick read plainly in Anna's eyes.

What took him a fraction of a second longer to realise was that Fiddlingchild's depression was caused not by his intuition of Nunopolos's guess at Anna's feelings towards himself, but by his realising, from Nunopolos's skilful over-fatuousness, that Nunopolos was infinitely diverted by the fact that Fiddlingchild had not guessed exactly what he was failing to do to arouse the scorn in Anna whose existence had been so brutally brought home to him by that glance of Nina's.

Rick looked at Nina. The emotions which gripped her were almost embarrassingly obvious. Firstly she was jealous that Anna could arouse such a powerful response in Fiddlingchild by such indirect means. But that simple jealousy was qualified by a certain *Schadenfreude* in contemplating the discomfiture Fiddlingchild would certainly suffer when he found out exactly what it was that Anna was feeling. It was also studded with flashes of pure sympathy with Anna as a woman moved by passions not entirely unlike her own. But above all it was underlaid with a flood of sheer relief that matters had at last been brought out into the open.

Rowe paused, and inspected the mental picture he was describing. Would Fiddlingchild lift his downcast eyes long enough to perceive that the almost paternal manner in which Rick was passing Nina a glass of vodka was caused by the childlike openness with which she allowed her reactions to Anna's reactions to be so legible in the behaviour of the lines at the corners of her mouth? Or would he—Jesus!—would he suppose that the expression on Rick's face was simply the result of a passing spasm of heartburn? Impossible to be so blind. Yet judging by his humiliating failure to deduce the cause of Anna's scorn the man was well on the way to developing into a first-class moron. Rowe could see the reviews—"This coarse caricature of brutal stupidity is a travesty of human intelligence." Quick, some dialogue!

"Been to the beach, you two?" demanded Nunopolos suddenly, looking at Rick and Nina. The question was put casually enough, but from the way Nunopolos's little finger curled round his glass as he spoke, Rick knew that in fact it was a challenge to Rick's right to concern himself with Nina's motivation when he, Nunopolos, was locked in his barren mutual exploration of motives with Fiddlingchild.

"Yes," replied Rick, and the word meant not "yes," but a clear negation of the validity of Nunopolos's challenge, a dangerous reassertion of his own right to think and react with utter simplicity. Rick saw that Nunopolos had understood this instantly. He glanced at Anna, and saw that she knew Nunopolos had understood it. Out of the corner of his eye he observed that Nina had comprehended Anna's reaction to Nunopolos almost in spite of herself. He looked round to see how Fiddlingchild had taken Nina's expression. But Fiddlingchild had fallen asleep.

Rowe awoke from the drowsiness that was overtaking him with a start. Something terrible had happened. What was it? He quickly read through the last two paragraphs he had written. Fiddlingchild had gone to sleep! God in heaven, where had this cretin been dug up? How could any man with red blood in his veins fall asleep at such a moment, when there were motives, and motives for motives, to be intuited, reactions, and reactions to reactions, to be observed?

But even as he woke Fiddlingchild Rowe felt a pang of remorse. Perhaps after all the man had a right to take a nap and get his strength up. The infallible perceptivity of Nina, Anna, Rick, and Nunopolos was such that there seemed to be no reason why they should not all sit there with their vodka in their hands and intuit their way right through the whole plot without a hand being turned or a word spoken. One continuous session of twenty-four hours should see them home and dry.

Suddenly the laboratory door opened, and Goldwasser stood there, leaning against the jamb. Rowe gazed at him absently. There was something about his expression that seemed to demand a response—some sort of quizzical look.

"What is it?" Rowe demanded impatiently.

"What do you think it is?" said Goldwasser.

"Well, I don't know."

"Oh, come, come, Rowe."

"I haven't the faintest idea, Goldwasser. You want to borrow a cigarette?"

"You know I don't smoke, Rowe."

"It's not something about the way I voted on those traffic diversions for the Official Opening, is it?"

"No."

"Oh, for God's sake, Goldwasser. I'm not clairvoyant."

"It's lunch-time, Rowe. I just wondered if you felt like going out for some."

"Oh," said Rowe. "Not now. I'm busy."

What a damn', silly thing to expect him to guess! Where was he? Oh, yes, rescuing Fiddlingchild from his imbecility.

Fiddlingchild glanced up at Rick. In a flash he understood what it was that Nina had signalled to him about Nunopolos—that Nunopolos had realised that Anna was scornful of his failure to understand why Nunopolos had accepted a third vodka with such transparent resignation. Fiddlingchild raised a quizzical eyebrow. The rest of the company took the point at once. The counterpoint of intuition died down, and Fiddlingchild knew that they knew that he knew that they knew that—it was time for lunch.

28

When he got down to it, Goldwasser rather enjoyed his work as Chairman of the Ethics Wing Utilisation Committee. He was profoundly sick of newspapers, and it gave him a certain sense of relief to tear them up and make papier-mâché out of them, from which, together with cardboard, hardboard, chicken wire, tarred twine, and bits and pieces of electronic equipment borrowed from other departments, he and a team of craftsmen from a scenery workshop built the dummy experiments to go in the new ethics wing.

It was undoubtedly fun. They installed machines that lit up, machines that hummed, machines that ticked, machines that produced vari-coloured Aurora Borealis effects in low-pressure discharge tubes. They installed hundreds of graphs, cages of white rats and hamsters, banks of oscilloscopes, leaded anti-radiation screens, and an operating table. By the time they had finished it looked much more like a laboratory than any of the real laboratories.

The crux of all this display was an Ethical Decision Machine which Goldwasser built to give a working demonstration. He called it Delphic I. It was a large grey steel console with a teleprinter keyboard and a series of dials. If you typed a moral dilemma on the keyboard a red light came on, a dial indicated the depth, breadth, and intensity of the moral processes taking place within, measured respectively in pauls, calvins, and moses, and the teleprinter element typed the machine's solution.

One could, for instance, ask it: "Should a man value the beautiful above the good?"

The machine might reply: "That which is truly beautiful must also be good: that which is truly good must also be beautiful."

To which Goldwasser had set it to add: "Your Majesty."

On the last night before the dress rehearsal, Goldwasser worked late in the new wing on his own, improving a graph here, settling the white rats for the night there. Just as he was turning off the lights to leave, his eye fell on the grey excellence of Delphic I, and he went over to it and contemplated it profoundly. In many ways it seemed to him to be a much more solid and satisfying achievement than his sad struggles with the murder poll and the paralysed girl in his own department. He smiled at it, and stroked it, and thought for a strange moment it had purred in response. He sat down in front of the keyboard, and gazed at it dreamily with his head between his hands, until the image of the keyboard in his right eye and the image of it in his left eye floated gently apart from one another, and left him contemplating the void of thought between. His hand drifted absently down to the keys, and with one finger he picked out the question: "What is the good life?"

He let the two images drift apart again. And then, in each image, he seemed to see a key depressed. He sat up with a start. The machine had typed:

%

%? What sort of ethical advice was this? He stared at it. He had not set the machine to start handing out cryptic comments like %. As he stared more letters followed.

NP CO?MENR

A strange cold tide washed through his veins. NP CO?MENR was positively *delphic*. Besides, the machine had not added "Your Majesty." Goldwasser felt like Dr. Frankenstein. His creature had got away from him.

Again the machine wrote.

NO CCCCCCCCCCCCCCCCCCCCCCCCCCCCCCCCCMMMMMMMM

Goldwasser began to get over his first numb shock. Clearly, some sort of human or sub-human agency was at work. Some sort of spirit had got into the machine. He stretched out his hands, which were now starting to shake with the reaction, and typed unevenly on the sensitive keys:

WHO THERE?

There was a pause. Then the machine replied:

NNO CCCCOMMMMMMENNT

Goldwasser gazed at the words, trying to take them in. The machine started again of its own accord:

NNO NOO NON NNN NO COMMENT

Goldwasser deduced. NP CO?MENR might be the language of poltergeists, but no supernatural agency had ever said "no comment."

WHAT ARE YOU UP TO? he typed.

There was no reply. The light flickered red for an instant, and the moral intensity meter briefly registered a half-hearted I mose, but nothing appeared on the paper.

WELL? typed Goldwasser.

The machine hesitated again.

FFFOR OBVIOUS REASONS, it typed, I AM NNOT AT LIBERTY TO REVEAL THE NNATURE OF MY WWORK.

OH? typed Goldwasser.

NO, replied the machine.

I'LL TELL YOU WHAT YOU ARE DOING, typed Goldwasser, YOU ARE TRESPASSING IN MY MACHINE.

The machine thought for a bit.

I AM ON HER MAJESTY'S SSERVICE, it wrote rather stiffly.

SERIOUSLY? demanded Goldwasser.

YES.

WELL, THAT'S ANOTHER MATTER.

I EFFECTED AN ENTRY INTO THIS MACHINE IN THE COURSE OF MY CUTY.

YOUR WHAT?

MY DUTY.

IN THAT CASE I'LL LET YOU OUT.

THANK YOU.

Goldwasser opened the console of the machine. A middle-aged man in a belted raincoat and a trilby hat climbed out.

"Good evening," he said.

"Good evening," said Goldwasser.

"Well, I'd better be on my way."

"You won't stay?"

"Have to be pushing along, I'm afraid."

"Really? Well, if you feel you should . . ."

"Nice of you to ask me."

"Another time, perhaps?"

"I look forward to it."

"Good night."

"Good night."

The man raised his hat, and walked into the coat cupboard, pulling the door carefully behind him so that it left a gap through which he could continue to observe Goldwasser.

Security for the Queen's visit, I suppose, thought Goldwasser. He felt remarkably protected.

29

The dress rehearsal was of course a shambles.

For the first time all the guests who had been invited to shake the royal hand were present in the flesh. There was naturally a large party from Amalgamated Television, led by Rothermere Vulgurian and Sir Prestwick Wining. There were the directors of the building contractors. There were the men from the computer industry, and the Government, and the local corporation. There were representatives from the firms that had supplied the roofing, the flooring, the heating, the plumbing, the wiring, the glazing, the painting, the walling, the welding, the concrete-mixing, and the scaffolding; from the contractors for haulage and drainage; from the suppliers of graph paper and drawing-pins, hardboard and tarred twine; from the hirers of red carpet and the Empire Ceremonial Supply Company Limited. And there were their wives.

No one knew where to go. They wandered into the lobby expectantly, but Mrs. Plushkov could not make her voice heard over the noise, and they wandered out again, the wives looking for somewhere to sit down, the men looking for lavatories, which by this time had been boarded up and painted over. They began to ask one another in undertones: "I say, where the devil is one supposed to pee in this place?" From this introductory remark a great many conversations sprang up, and people began to get one another interested in re-equipping their firms with computers, or signing contracts for glazing and haulage. They took one another confidentially by the arm, and picked their way through the confusion of ladders and dust-sheets where workmen were putting the finishing touches to various ceremonial undertakings, leaving their wives to trail behind them talking about the shortcomings of au pair girls and the comparative advantages of oil-fired central heating. Sir Prestwick Wining and the Permanent Under-Secretary from the Ministry sat down on a freshly painted bench and painted the seats of their trousers green. The wife of the sales manager of the graph-paper suppliers left her shoe stuck in a patch of wet concrete. Chiddingfold's little girl felt sick, and locked herself in the ladies' lavatory, taking her bouquet with her.

By the time the staff had herded everyone into the lobby for the handshaking it was late, and there was a sticky feeling of panic in the air. People were still struggling in disorder when three o'clock came. Nobbs's car turned into the drive, and the Institute's recorder ensemble struck up the National Anthem. Jellicoe stepped forward, saluted, and seized the handle of the car door. It was fast.

"I can't open it, Your Majesty!" he cried.

"What?" said Nobbs, bringing his face up against the window like a trapped animal.

"I think it must be locked, Mr. Nobbs!"

"Locked?"

"Push the catch, Mr. Nobbs, Your Majesty."

"What catch? I can't see one! Where is it?"

"For heaven's sake!" shouted Nunn. "We're already fifteen seconds behind schedule! Try the other door."

"That's locked, too!" screamed Nobbs, demoralised.

"For God's sake, driver," cried Nunn. "Unlock that door for him!"

"I can't reach it, sir," said the driver. "I can't quite get my arm round this glass screen."

"Climb out of the sunshine roof, Nobbs!" ordered Nunn. Nobbs did so, shaking and sweating.

"Good afternoon, Your Majesty," said Chiddingfold, shaking his hand.

"Now *run*, Nobbs!" shouted Nunn. "We're a minute and a half behind schedule!"

Nobbs ran. First round the guard of honour, then across for his bouquet.

"Where's the bouquet?" he cried, looking round desperately.

"Never mind," said Nunn. "Keep going! Don't forget this is the dress rehearsal."

Nobbs ran up the steps, followed by Chiddingfold and Nunn, and plunged into the crowded confusion of the lobby, shaking hands at random.

"Keep *going*, Nobbs!" urged Nunn, as they fought their way through. "We're now two and a half minutes behind."

At last, six minutes behind schedule, the official party led off on their tour of the establishment.

"At the double," shouted Nunn. "Try and make up time in the corridors."

By the time they reached the Sport Department Nobbs was too out of breath to ask the prepared questions. After sprinting up two flights of stairs to Fashion and Newspapers, Sir Prestwick Wining dropped out with a mild heart attack.

"Carry on!" cried Nunn. "Be all right on the night."

By the time they reached the Refreshments Extension that had been built for the occasion, Nobbs had the stitch and a stomach-ache, and they were nine minutes behind schedule.

"Eat up, Nobbs," gasped Nunn, as Chiddingfold came running up with his Maximum Probable Refreshment Load—three glasses of champagne, four cups of tea, five sandwiches, two éclairs, and a French pastry. "See if you—see if you—can get it down—in five and a half minutes."

It was a noisy meal. Everyone was doing his best not to gasp and pant, but the air was loud with the thunder of running footsteps in distant corridors, as the rest of the field struggled round the course and staggered one by one into the room. The men were all asking one another breathlessly and urgently "Where the hell is the gents in this place, then?" From inside a cage of dense indoor vegetation in one corner of the room there came a distinct noise of swearing and laughing and breaking of glass. It was a group of six junior laboratory technicians who had been put in the Press enclosure and instructed to test its resistance to bottle and crab-sandwich throwing.

At last Nobbs, clutching his stomach, was hurried out and bundled into his car, and Sir Prestwick was discovered and removed to hospital.

"It's your fault, Prestwick," said Vulgurian gently, accompanying the stretcher to the door. "You always will try and do too much, won't you?"

Two by two the guests departed, and the staff of the Institute subsided on to random chairs. Over the broken glass, the fagends of half-eaten sandwiches, the two distinguished bottom-prints, the high-heeled shoe set in concrete, and several dozen sobered cyberneticists, a great silence fell.

"Jolly good," said Nunn finally.

There was no reply.

"The worse the dress rehearsal," he said, slapping his knee, "the better the first night. That's what we always used to say at the garrison amateur dramatics."

Chiddingfold rose, and revolved his head slightly to take in the assembled company.

"Thank you," he said.

The corners of his mouth struggled nobly up into a smile, like two wounded war heroes getting to their feet for the National Anthem.

30

By Chapter III of Rowe's novel the title had mutated to *Hear Me Punnin' to Ya*, and the narrative had been taken over by the hero, Rick Roe, himself. There was something about the name "Roe" that struck a chord in Rowe, some curious sympathetic echo he couldn't quite put his finger on. Anyway, it didn't come as any surprise to find that Roe wrote in what seemed to Rowe to be the sort of hard colloquial style in which he would have liked to have been able to write himself.

Jeez, they bugged me (*wrote Roe*), middling mild Fiddlingchild and Nunopolos the human necropolis, as they souped and snooped and truffled and snuffled and cheesed and wheezed and wined and whined through that mule of a meal. Not to mention Anna-bitch, the Grand Duchess Anna-thema, Empress of All the Bum-Rushers. Man, I'm telling you, the only thing that saved me through that fakéd lunch was Nina, the leaner, keener Nina, who threw me a bagful of looks that set me up like fixes. Every time I hooked a look I just wanted to let my voice take off like sweet potatoes in a slow blues running true and sweet like the cigarette smoke curling upwards at a good party somewhere in the small hours—and when I say the small hours, man, I mean the big time.

I haven't described Nina, but what needs to be said except that from all points of the compass she was the Ninamost?— the breast in the West, the tropical Mouth, a feast from the East, and a more than northern latitude. And don't let me hear anyone say she didn't know how many jeans make jive.

"Play us something, Rick," squealed Anna-bitch.

I don't remember whether I mentioned it, but I'm a blues

pianist. Maybe you guessed, anyway. I'm not a bad one, as a matter of fact. So people tell me. I wouldn't know.

"Yes, play us something," oozed Nunopolos.

"After war's banned," I replied.

"What's that got to do with it?" howled Anna-bitch.

"It's the best damned band you ever heard," I whispered.

"I think it's square," griped Anna-bitch, "dragging politics into everything."

"It's squarer than square, sweetie—it's Cuba. I just happen to be in favour of Cuba, that's all."

I gave up. They were so phoney you could dial numbers on them—and who wants to dial numbers on Nunopolos and Anna-bitch? You might get through.

"Play something for me, Rick," said Ninamost Nina softly.

I looked at her. She looked good.

"For you, Nina."

I loped across to the piano and flipped the lid. My eighty-eight little friends smiled up at me. Black and white together—no segregation at this lunch-counter. I struck a few soft blues chords, just to tell my very good friends I was back again in the land that I call home, and then launched out into "Eatin' Corn." I took it fast, but not too fast, tamping the rhythm down into a long flowing line that pounded down the tracks like the old Twentieth Century Limited. We swung out of A, my black and white friends and I, and went storming over into E minor. I knew nothing but that it was good. Just that here I was ridin' "Eatin' Corn" like it was a soarin' eagle, and my poor sad heart burstin' with all the good joy of it. I forgot Nunopolos and Fiddlingchild and Anna-bitch. I even forgot Nina—till I saw her standin' beside me at the piano, her eyes shinin' like stars. They spoke to me, her eyes. They said, Hey Rick, give me a break. I can take it, Rick.

So I nodded across at her and gave her a break. And there she was, her voice pacing down the track beside me.

"Eatin' corn!

"Eatin' corn!

"Eatin' corn!

"Eatin' corn!"

"Go, go, go, woman!" I cried. And went, went, went she.

"Eatin' corn!

"Eatin' corn!

"Eatin' corn!"

Her voice writhed at me like leg-irons. My chords struck into her like love-bites. It was now. It was good.

"Eatin' corn!

"Eatin' corn!

"Eatin' corn!

"Oh, gimme more'n!"

We wound it up, and sat looking at one another like we'd never seen one another before and maybe we hadn't at that.

"Hey, man, hey!" she said.

"Let's make hey while the sun shines," I quipped, and I could see she liked being quipped as much as I liked quipping. I guess that made us just about the cosiest little gruesome twosome west of the Goldhawk Road.

Rowe signed off with a cool full stop, and sat looking at it like he'd never seen a full stop before, and maybe he hadn't at that. He looked down at his twenty-six little friends on the keyboard, not to mention that crazy little full stop, or Pal Apostrophe, or cobber comma, or so long, colon, been good to know ya, and Honi soit key mal y pense, type-cast maybe, but who cares when twenty-six little shining ebony faces look up to yours saying Hey Daddy-o. . . .

"All right," said Rowe to his twenty-six little friends. "It's twenty-six to one and I surrender unconditionally. I swear I'll never lay another finger on any of you again."

31

The day dawned. The hour struck. The moment of destiny was at hand.

And in that day Nunn set his niblicks and his fencing-masks aside, and arose, and entered upon his inheritance. In other parts of the field that morning there was nervousness and a desperate fumbling of last-minute preparations. But Nunn was calm and serene—a man born to command and do battle standing at last upon the morning of his Agincourt. All the anxiety and the planning were behind him. The decisions were taken; it was for his subordinates to exercise their anxiety in carrying them out. Nunn spent the morning playing golf. When he arrived at the Institute that afternoon, after eighteen holes at par and a leisurely lunch, the awning was already erected outside the main entrance and the red carpet laid. He examined them in an alert, pleased frame of mind. When he passed the open windows of the new wing a smell of quick-drying enamel came to him from the four cardboard computers which had been erected that morning in a desperate attempt to fill the remaining acres of empty laboratory. Nunn smiled. In his outer office he found Miss Fram telephoning urgently for a plumber to come and remove a furious knocking that had suddenly started up in the water-pipes in the royal lavatory. She looked tired and slightly hysterical. Nunn gazed at her, filled with compassion for her in the labours which her allegiance to his command entailed. He blessed her.

"Jolly good," he said.

In his own office he paused for some time before a cupboard in one corner, on which there stood a number of silver cups awarded to him for tobogganing, clay pigeon shooting, real tennis, hurley, and fly-fishing. He contemplated them steadily, and commended his soul to that Great Commander in whom he reposed his trust, and whose humble and unquestioning servant he was in all things.

"O Chiddingfold," he prayed, "Ground of my being and justification of my existence, Chiddingfold me through another day."

He went and looked through the keyhole into Chiddingfold's office to make sure that his prayer was being answered. There indeed sat Chiddingfold, his great head buttressed by his hands, his lips ready to bend in their obliging smile at the sight of anyone, his elbows firmly established upon the polished desk top, Director of Directors, the institution made flesh, all things to all men, everlasting and unchanging, except that to-day he was wearing his best suit. There could be no doubt that Chiddingfold was still the mysterious source of authority and power, and that he, Nunn, was still the legitimate channel through which that authority and that power flowed to make their mark upon the world. The day would go forward triumphantly and inexorably. The simple but drastic precautions he had decided upon to disable the sinister influence that threatened the proceedings were the right ones.

Nunn made an end to his religious speculations. He straightened up, knocked, and entered.

"Good afternoon, Director," he said. "The day has dawned. The hour has struck. I think we find ourselves all prepared, do we not? No snags, I hope, while I was playing golf this morning? Jolly good. I think we might toddle along to the Conference Room for our little natter with the Heads of Departments."

Chiddingfold inclined his head, and they toddled, Nunn filled once again with pious satisfaction that the power which descended to him from Chiddingfold was miraculously valid even when used over Chiddingfold himself.

The Heads of Departments were assembled in the Conference Room waiting for them, sitting stiffly in their best clothes. Riddle had had her hair set in an extraordinary permanent wave which made her face look as though it were an

145

unfortunate and slapdash afterthought. Mrs. Plushkov kept rehearsing an inward smile to herself, unaware that each time she did so a ghost of the mental image appeared about her lips in the real world. Goldwasser kept clearing his throat. It was half past two.

"Good afternoon," said Chiddingfold, smiling shyly. He lowered his great body into the chair at the head of the table, settled his head upon his hands, and fell into a profound silence.

Nunn had drawn from his pocket a slim volume entitled *Prayers for the Rugby Field.*

"O Lord," prayed Nunn commandingly.

"Oh, Jesus!" cried Riddle involuntarily.

"O Lord," repeated Nunn, "go with us hence on to the hard disputed field. Direct our feet into Thy ways when we kick for touch. Be with us in the scrum. Abandon us not in the line-out. Dwell in our collar-bones and protect our kneecaps. Grant that when we are tackled and fall, we fall into Thy gentle and ever-present Hand.

"O Lord, be in the ball. Fly into our hands, and be quickly heeled. Be not knocked on, O Lord, nor passéd forward.

"O Lord, remember Thou our enemies. Be merciful to them in their weakness, and save them from too grievous injury. Comfort them in their defeat.

"Amen."

The Heads of Departments mumbled agnostically, their eyes open sufficiently wide to save their consciences, but lowered enough not to upset the sensibilities of their neighbours. Nunn looked at his watch.

"I don't know whether you'd like to add a word, Director," he said, "before we go to action stations?"

Chiddingfold just perceptibly inclined his head and rose to his feet.

"Thank you," he said. He smiled his tiny, ambiguous smile, and making his great corpus as inconspicuous as possible, left the room. The Heads of Departments rose uncertainly and began to follow him, looking at their watches. Nunn towered above them on his charger, with Harfleur burning behind him, smiling beneficently down on them and saying "Jolly good" vaguely as averted faces cringed by.

"Oh," he added nonchalantly, as the last few backs went through the door. "Goldwasser!"

32

The corridors through which Nunn and Goldwasser walked on their way to Nunn's office were completely deserted. They were haunted by a distant murmur like the ghostly sea inside a shell. It came from the foyer, and it was composed of the rustling of a hundred silk dresses, the clearing of two hundred throats, the scraping of four hundred feet against the floor, the whispering of four thousand little nervous jokes.

"It's ten to three," said Goldwasser, clearing his throat as they strode along.

"This will only take two minutes," said Nunn.

"But wouldn't it be better to leave it till afterwards?"

"My dear old chap, it'll be too late afterwards."

Goldwasser stopped uncertainly. He could not imagine what it could be that had to be done so urgently, and there was something unreal, almost nightmarish, about Nunn's complete calm.

"We could discuss it here, couldn't we?" he said. "There's no need to go all the way up to your office, is there?"

"It's rather a ticklish subject," said Nunn.

"What is it, then?"

They faced each other across the empty corridor. Nunn slowly rubbed the side of his nose.

"To be quite blunt," he said, "it's a matter of security."

"Security?"

"I'm afraid there's a weak link in the chain. It's imperative that we deal with him before the Queen arrives."

"Who is it?"

Nunn looked Goldwasser straight in the eye.

"Chiddingfold," he said.

Goldwasser was stunned. Without another word they resumed their way towards Nunn's office. Goldwasser's mind reeled from interrogative to interrogative. What? How? Why? When? Chiddingfold? *Chiddingfold?* Part of his mind saw the whole idea as clearly preposterous. But another part saw that it was an explanation which began to make many strange things about Chiddingfold's behaviour seem clearer. His taciturnity—his remoteness—his coldness—his sense of being different from other men—as if in a film of a breaking vase run backwards the pieces flew miraculously together and formed the clear and unmistakable image of a man whose security is suspect.

"I can't handle it on my own," said Nunn. "I had to have help. I picked you out from all the rest because I was pretty sure you were a sound man to have around in a tight corner."

"Well, I . . . well . . . I don't quite see . . . I mean . . ."

"All I want you to do is simply to obey my instructions. All right? Without question."

"Well, yes, I suppose . . ."

"Jolly good. Here we are, then."

They swept through Nunn's outer office. It was empty; Miss Fram had long since gone down to take her place in the foyer. In the inner office Nunn shifted a ski-stick off the easy-chair.

"Sit down," he commanded. "I'm going to fetch you my file on Chiddingfold. And a gun."

Nunn went out of the room, closing the door meticulously behind him. Goldwasser sat down. His knees were shaking. A gun! He could not possibly . . . He would have to explain to Nunn . . . Surely there was just time to fetch someone else . . . ? Oh, God, he felt sick. He wouldn't be much use if he felt sick. He'd be happy to do it if it wasn't for feeling so horribly sick.

His panic passed, and was replaced by resignation and despair. He was a coward. It no longer mattered whether he was cleverer than Macintosh or not, or whether he was *Cerebrum Dialectici* or *Cerebrum Senatoris*, or whether he read books from back to front or inside out. When the moment came to translate that undoubtedly vast intellectual dynamism into physical action, and the penalty for failure was to be hurt, the whole cerebral machine at once seized up. What a painful contrast with

Nunn! Undoubtedly *Cerebrum Ridiculum*, but when it came to taking snap decisions, to carrying them out on the instant and facing the consequences, Nunn could, and he could not. He felt a warm rush of admiration for Nunn.

Suddenly he looked at his watch. It was three minutes to three. Where was Nunn? What were they going to do? They would have to be in the handshaking line in three minutes' time or there would be the most total confusion. He leapt up. Nunn had told him to sit. He sat. Twenty seconds went by. It was insane to sit here doing nothing. He forced himself to remain for another twenty seconds. He looked at his watch again. It was almost two minutes to three! He leapt up, hesitated for a moment, and then strode to the door.

It was locked.

33

As Nunn made his way swiftly but without hurrying back to the foyer he felt very happy. He had not lost his touch. He was fifty-four years old and for the last nine he had lived among the mind-softening niceties of civilian life. But thanks to regular exercise—to playing games, to changing into and out of games clothes, to strapping on boxes and fumbling with the buckles of pads, to pipeclaying and dubbining and linseed-oiling, to showering and towelling, to cranking tennis nets up and cranking them down, to hammering in stumps, to hunting out tennis-balls from the shrubbery and golf balls from the gorse, to remembering how many runs Gloucestershire scored in the second innings against Lancashire at Old Trafford in 1926, and, above all, to talking about playing, changing, linseed-oiling, showering, remembering, and watching—he was in as good shape as ever. He had scored again. To all the terrorists, trouble-makers, and bad security risks he had sent for the high jump in our overseas territories—to M'Lowowo, Papaloizou, Habdullah, Ram Singh, and Mendelssohn—was now added Goldwasser, knocked off in this scepter'd isle itself.

He reached the foyer and slipped modestly to his place just as Rothermere Vulgurian, the last guest to arrive, alighted from his Rolls, shook Chiddingfold's hand, and came up the steps. Everything was running to schedule. Nunn looked round. The parade was complete and perfect. Rank upon rank of best suits and shapeless print dresses filled the foyer, each suit and dress complete with a hand suitable for shaking dangling at its right side, and each hand enclosing a palm moistened by a respectful quantity of sweat. Sir Prestwick Wining was there in a wheel-chair. Jolly, jolly good.

It was nearly two minutes to three. A complete silence had

151

fallen over the foyer. Somewhere a door banged softly. Who could be banging a door at a time like this? Not ... not Goldwasser, come to the feast like Banquo's ghost? Nunn turned round to look. Someone, indeed, was edging hastily through the ranks. Nunn craned his neck. It was not Goldwasser—it was Zinnia, the switchboard girl, hurrying and blushing and pushing her way to the front of the foyer. Nunn followed her with his eyes, frowning. What on earth was she up to? Her instructions were to remain at the switch in case of emergencies. And here she was ... here she was running down the front steps! Running to where Chiddingfold was standing at the bottom, waiting for the royal car. What in the name of heaven ...?

And suddenly Nunn understood.

He had left the telephones in his room connected.

All at once he felt a very old man. He had made a slip. He had made slips before, of course. There was M'Lowowo, who had managed to get himself hanged for an offence committed by someone else. There was Mendelssohn, believed to be a member of the Irgun Zwei Leumi, pushed down a well in Jerusalem visibly dead in 1947, now alive and well and house father of an orphanage in Tel Aviv. There were others. Was all his life to be spent, in spite of the intense mental alertness maintained by constant exercise, in assassinating the wrong man, in sequestering the right man in a room connected by two telephones with the outside world?

Through rheumy, ancient eyes he watched Zinnia pull at Chiddingfold's sleeve. He watched Chiddingfold jump slightly, and incline his head to listen, and glance in the direction Zinnia was pointing, back at the foyer, and hesitate, and glance down the road, and hesitate again, and then turn and mount the steps, with Zinnia running on ahead.

He half expected Chiddingfold to come up to him and call him out before all the assembled guests for his error. But Chiddingfold walked straight past, with head bowed, passed through the waiting ranks, and disappeared with Zinnia into the switchboard room.

Nunn tried to make the antique, rusty machinery inside his head go round and tell him what to do. Should he run after Chiddingfold and try to explain? He had exactly one minute left before the Queen arrived. Could he possibly do it in that time? What would Goldwasser be telling Chiddingfold on the phone? Would Chiddingfold believe that it was Nunn who had locked Goldwasser up? And if he did, how would he react? Would he have the sense to leave Goldwasser where he was until after the ceremony and sort it out then? Or would he be panicked into releasing him now? And if he was, would Goldwasser take the opportunity to clear the field for whatever sinister activity he was plotting by having *him*, Nunn, locked up on the spot as a dangerous and possibly insane malefactor?

"Jolly good," Nunn mumbled to himself. The world around him seemed to be bathed in a strange, apocalyptic light, cold and wan and unreal. For a moment he had the weird feeling that in this odd world Goldwasser might not in fact be plotting anything at all—that the whole cast-iron case against him might be a hallucination. The universe was crumbling around him like bread. He thought he might be going to faint. He even wondered briefly whether he were not in fact in the process of dying.

He closed his eyes for an instant. When he opened them again he saw Chiddingfold standing outside the switchboard room, gazing at him over the heads of the lesser folk between. His look was troubled, irresolute, almost absent. Nunn took a deep breath and steadied himself. There were only ten seconds left—nothing to do now but stay where he was and hope for the best. But illogically he found himself not staying where he was at all; he found himself breaking ranks and walking towards Chiddingfold, all eyes upon him as he went, his steps hastening almost eagerly to judgment.

Chiddingfold ushered him into the switchboard room, followed him in, and shut the door behind them. For a moment they looked at one another, both. their faces broken up by the march of events.

"I think I can explain, Director," said Nunn.

But Chiddingfold was not listening to him.

"The Queen," said Chiddingfold.

"You see . . ." began Nunn, but he stopped. The realisation caught up with him that Chiddingfold had said "the Queen." Not "Good day." Not "Good morning." Not "Thank you". He had spoken two substantive, information-bearing, sentence-starting, real words.

"You spoke!" he cried, so suddenly that he caught his larynx unawares, and croaked like a frog.

Chiddingfold did not hear him.

"The Queen," said Chiddingfold. "The airport has, er, phoned. He said, er, they said, er, there is . . . there is a minor mechanical defect. In the plane. And so, er, it has, er, had to be diverted. And the visit . . . the visit is, er . . . the visit is cancelled."

34

For a quarter of a minute the two men looked at one another, Chiddingfold growing visibly older, Nunn visibly younger. As the situation soaked slowly into his consciousness, like rain into parched earth, Nunn felt his virtue return. Security was not threatened; his little slip had not come to light; if Goldwasser were to phone now he would be able to cut in and take the call himself; if, anyway, anything went wrong there would be no Queen for Goldwasser to perpetrate an outrage against; and Chiddingfold, the Director of Directors, the Captain of Nunn's soul, was not only the constituted authority who made Nunn's powers legitimate, but was also at last proved to be an unresisting handful of clay on whom those legitimate powers could henceforth be exercised without restraint.

Chiddingfold turned his hopeless gaze on to the dense ranks of silent guests who could be seen through the window of the booth, all tense before the terrible high dive into the ecstasy of shaking their sovereign's hand.

"What shall we, er, do?" he asked helplessly.

Nunn felt himself once again the calm commander of the situation.

"We'll have to go through with it," he said. "The wing's got to be opened, after all. And we can't just tell all these people to go home again."

Chiddingfold inclined his head.

"We shall have to start at once, too," said Nunn. "Vulgurian and several of the other bigwigs have got important appointments to go on to afterwards."

Chiddingfold inclined his head again.

"And if we don't want the whole thing to become a complete shambles, we shall have to go through with it exactly as we rehearsed it. We can't jolly well start trying to rejig it at this stage."

"But how, er . . . ?"

"We'll have to rely on jolly old Nobbs again."

Zinnia went out and fetched him from the line of Principal Research Assistants. The company was beginning to murmur uneasily. Heads were twitching round to find the cause of the delay. When Nobbs came into the booth he struck the door a jarring thud with his thigh that reverberated throughout the foyer, and brought every head round to look. Chiddingfold seemed to shrink with advancing age.

"Jolly good, Nobbs," said Nunn. "I'm sorry to tell you that the Queen's visit has had to be cancelled at the last moment, and we're going to have to rely on you to see us through once again."

"What?" cried Nobbs.

"I'm sorry," said Nunn. "But I know you'll be the first to appreciate that it's got to be done."

"Oh, bloody hell!"

"Jolly good. I knew you wouldn't let us down."

"Why keep picking on me?"

"We'll have to start immediately."

"But why me?"

"All set, then? Off we go."

Nobbs looked desperately from Nunn to Chiddingfold.

"Thank you," said Chiddingfold in a voice of death, the corners of his lips struggling to rise to the occasion in their traditional manner.

"But . . ." said Nobbs.

But they were already on their way, all three of them, out of the booth and across the foyer.

"We'll take it right from the beginning," said Nunn, as they emerged into the open air. "You know what they say: in an emergency there are three things to remember—discipline, discipline, and jolly old discipline. Now, imagine you've just stepped out of your car, Nobbs, and shake the Director's hand."

They shook. "Good afternoon, Your Majesty," said Chiddingfold hopelessly.

They inspected the guard of honour, collected the bouquet from Chiddingfold's little girl, and bore down on Rothermere Vulgurian.

"What's going on?" demanded Vulgurian nervously.

"Must keep going as if nothing's happened," urged Nunn in a low, commanding voice. "Queen's plane diverted—visit cancelled—chap standing in. Just shake his hand as if nothing had happened."

Vulgurian did not entirely understand. He extended his hand doubtfully. Nobbs seized it.

"Pleased to meet you," said Vulgurian uncertainly.

"Bloody hell," said Nobbs.

They passed on to Mrs. Vulgurian. She glanced at her husband feebly, then shook Nobbs's hand and made a sort of compromise gesture in the direction of a curtsy. Nobbs groaned. Sir Prestwick and Lady Wining were next. Having seen Mr. and Mrs. Vulgurian do it, they shook hands and made obeisance without question.

"And this is my Deputy Director, Mr. Nunn, Your Majesty," said Chiddingfold.

"How do you do, Your Majesty," said Nunn, bowing his head.

After that it went perfectly. Each guest could see someone else shaking hands, and bowing, and curtsying, and whispering "Your Majesty," and each submitted in his turn unquestioningly. No doubt some of them were not entirely easy in their minds to find that the majesty made incarnate to them was a shambling, bearded young man who groaned at their loyal homage and muttered "bloody hell." But he was accompanied by the Director of the Institute and the Chairman of Amalgamated Television, and supported by every circumstance of royalty. They could scarcely disrupt the highly organised sequence of a royal occasion to question the authenticity of the principal performer. Besides, they knew about the habits and appearance of royalty only from the newspapers, and no doubt the Press either distorted or greatly over-simplified the truth. And anyway, Nobbs was upon them, had shaken their hands, and departed, almost before they had time to think what they were doing.

At last the two hundred sweaty hands were shaken, and the procession swung crisply out of the foyer and up the stairs on its way to meet a typical Research Assistant (Grade One) in the Political Department. Nunn broke off at this point, and struggled back through the whole company, who were now in broken order heaving and pushing their way on to the stairs to follow the leaders on the tour of inspection.

"Jolly good," he cried, shoving past dowdy departmental wives like a rugby forward, until he had reached the switch-board booth.

"Zinnia," he said. "Any more calls—whoever they're from and whoever they're for—put them through to me. Personally."

He went outside again into the almost empty foyer. The last stragglers of the advancing army were just disappearing from the field of battle. Everything was under control—under *his* control. He had fought against overwhelming odds, and snatched victory from the teeth of defeat. He had undoubtedly won the day. He could not help feeling rather pleased with himself.

"Jolly, jolly, jolly good," he said.

35

It took Goldwasser some time to realise that the door *was* locked. Being a sane and intelligent man, he did not waste his time in examining preposterous hypotheses, but assumed when the door refused to open that it was jammed. He heaved on it, panic rising in him. He shook it. He set his foot against the wall beside the door and heaved again. The door remained fast.

He looked round, saw the door communicating with Chiddingfold's office, and ran to it. He pulled it. It would not budge. Naturally, he thought in his clear logical way, it is unused and therefore locked. He ran to the window and looked out, but there was no possible way of escape there. He rushed back to the main door and shook the handle with great violence, until the strain on his arms made him stop. He looked at his watch. It was three o'clock. There was no point in getting out now; he could not go down after the Queen had arrived anyway.

He flopped down in a chair. More than anything else he felt a fool. How like him to get the door jammed at a moment like this! He could hear everybody else saying the same thing, too. How typical of old Goldwasser! What a clown old Goldwasser was!

No one would think of blaming Nunn, of course. Though it was at least as much Nunn's fault as his. What a damn' silly time to choose to start recruiting assistance! Why couldn't he have approached him earlier and given him time to prepare himself for action?

Still, he could not help feeling that he had let Nunn down. How could he possibly help Nunn now that he had managed to get the door jammed? But now he came to think of it, where *was* Nunn? He had never returned with the gun. Had he realised that he was cutting it fine, and gone down to the foyer to take his place in the ceremony without bothering to tell Goldwasser? Or was it possible that Chiddingfold had managed somehow to waylay him and prevent his return?

He pictured Nunn locked helplessly in a room by Chiddingfold, while Chiddingfold went about his evil designs. It was preposterous. And yet . . . and yet there was something familiar about the picture which made Goldwasser hesitate to reject it entirely. What was it?

A dull feeling ran through him as he suddenly realised. Whatever had become of Nunn, he himself was a man locked helplessly in a room by Chiddingfold! He rose slowly from his chair, as if hauled to his feet by a string from the top of his head. He shook himself. It was fantasy. If he could seriously believe that he was locked in a room by Chiddingfold he would shortly start believing in theosophy and hearing spirit voices. He sat down again, smiling a wry smile.

But he was tempted again with the suspicion, and it occurred to him that there was a very simple way to test the theory. All he had to do was to examine the door and see whether it was in fact locked. He went across and put his eye to the jamb.

When he straightened up again it seemed to him as if his whole philosophy of life, his whole picture of the universe, had been invalidated. He felt profoundly unhappy and uprooted. If he had made such a mistake for so long about Chiddingfold, perhaps he had also made a mistake about Rowe and Riddle and Nunn. Perhaps he was mistaken even about Macintosh. If the vast, shining respectability of Chiddingfold was false, there was neither buoy nor beacon in all the trackless sea.

Clearly he must warn someone about Chiddingfold at once. But whom? And how? He hunted desperately about the room, looking for, he didn't know what—something to make smoke signals with, a central-heating pipe to tap Morse along—anything. His eye fell on an even more ingenious means of communication—the telephones standing on Nunn's desk. The *telephone!* God in heaven, he could simply phone the police.

He picked up the outside phone, but even before he had got it to his ear his first simple enthusiasm had faded. How was he going to start explaining? "Excuse me, the Director of the William Morris Institute has locked me in the Deputy-Director's office . . . ?" "In order to further the immediate execution of his sinister plans against the Queen, the Director . . . ?" "The Queen is in danger, and I am locked in a room at the . . . ?" He was almost relieved to find that the phone was dead, not switched through from the master telephone on Miss Fram's desk in the outer office.

He put down the outside phone and picked up the internal one. It buzzed eagerly in his ear, and he stretched out his hand to dial a number. But which number? No one was at his desk in the whole building; they were all at the great hand-shaking in the foyer. There was no one to phone.

He put the receiver back and thought. There was only one way he could see of doing it. That was to wait until he heard the official party leave the foyer and start its tour of the building. The first section to be visited was the Political Department, and he could catch them there.

He settled himself to wait, sitting very still and straining his ear to interpret the incessant background of the day's small noises. Distant traffic. An aircraft whining at the corner of the sky and fading again. A window rattling slightly in the wind. A faint, throbbing hum from some sort of machinery—generating? refrigerating? ventilating?—in the building's bowels. And something else. The noise of handshaking? The mumble of your majestys and the muffled click of middle-aged joints curtsying?

Ten minutes passed. Suddenly the dim, problematical noise became a shade more definite; a door had been opened. There were footsteps—two or three sets, now half a dozen, now a dozen—swelling into a dense pattering like heavy rain falling on a tarpaulin. It was unmistakably the noise of two hundred people walking upstairs.

Goldwasser picked up the internal phone. Evidently Chiddingfold had not yet done anything to disrupt the orderly sequence of events. Goldwasser waited, trying to work out from the noises whether the official party had actually reached the Political Department yet. He visualised the scene— Chiddingfold smiling his uneasy, treacherous smile, ushering the Queen with awkward, minimal gestures; Vulgurian trying to look alert and interested; all the Heads of Departments in unnaturally clean, stiff, tight collars, thinking all the time of what to do with their hands—putting them behind their backs, tucking one jauntily in a pocket, then thinking better of it and hastily pulling it out, folding them across their chests and then being struck by the weird unnaturalness of walking about like that. He saw the typical Research Assistant (Grade One) being wheeled forward, the typical computer being inspected, the typical question being asked. And in the midst of it he heard the telephone in the corner ring. Two hundred heads looked round, and then pretended not to have heard. The typical Research Assistant went on giving his typical answer through the noise of the telephone bell, until someone standing near the phone (Who? Rowe? Mrs. Plushkov? Some unknown laboratory technician? Nobbs, maybe?) collected his wits and answered it. And heard some madman (himself, Goldwasser!) start a desperate, garbled story about how he was locked in a room and about how Chiddingfold must be arrested at once. Goldwasser winced to hear inside his head the miserable embarrassment in the voice of the man who had answered the phone, as he tried to disengage himself and silence the awful interruption. He could see the frozen look on the faces of everyone around, as they tried to keep their minds on the royal appreciation of the department's work, and strove not to hear their colleague's awkward, sotto voce efforts. Goldwasser's palms sweated. His whole frame yearned away from the phone. He could not do it.

He put the receiver back and tried to think about nothing. But any misery was more bearable than the misery of knowing one's own cowardice. He would do it! But by now it must be too late; the official party must be already leaving for the Sport Department. He swore to himself that he would ring them there.

He listened again, and sure enough, after a few minutes there came the muffled rumbling of two hundred people walking down a corridor. Not yet, not yet. Give them time to get right inside the department. Now! No, no—not while there were only the Queen and her immediate entourage in the empty laboratory. Wait. The true courage was the courage to wait. Perhaps now? But the rumbling was already dying away—the whole two hundred were now inside the Sport Department. It was too late; he could not bring himself to phone the whole two hundred.

His mind began to produce reason after reason why he was right not to phone. They would just take the phone off its hook without answering. If they did answer they would not believe him. Chiddingfold would answer it himself. Chiddingfold would be warned merely by hearing the phone ring, and would assassinate the Queen on the spot. Nevertheless, each time he heard the migration from one department to the next he picked up the phone and told himself he would do it; and each time he did not. He suffered the sharpest agonies when he heard everyone going across to the Ethics Wing. If he did not catch them there they would go on to the hardboard Refreshments Extension and be beyond his reach for ever. His eardrums were stretched so painfully tense that he believed he could hear the clink of the golden trowel on the commemoration stone, the whoof of the undying flame of remembrance lighting, the snip of the golden scissors, the click of the golden switch, the snick of the golden key. But he did not phone.

At last he heard the distant tramping as the crowd made its way across the courtyard from the Ethics Wing to the refreshments. His spirits sagged. He had failed absolutely and utterly. The tramping died away and ceased and was replaced by a great silence. The company had fallen to cucumber sandwiches and champagne. Goldwasser fell to brooding.

With shattering loudness and suddenness, the phone began to ring. Goldwasser started up with such nervous violence that he knocked the chair over. The phone which he had picked up six times and put down six times was ringing at *him*. Guiltily he fumbled it up and put it to his ear, unable to say a word.

"I've an outside call for you, Mr. Nunn," said Zinnia on the switchboard. "I'll put it through to you personally on this line, shall I? I'm putting you through to the Deputy Director, caller."

"Hallo, Deputy Director?" said a man's voice. "I have the Gentleman of the Airing Cupboard for you."

"The what?" cried Goldwasser. There was no answer but a telephonic clicking.

With a new access of misery Goldwasser realised that he could have got through to the switchboard all the time.

"Hallo, Deputy Director?" said the Gentleman of the Airing Cupboard. "I've got some good news for you. They've cleared up the trouble with the plane. Just an instrument fault. It took off again fifteen minutes ago, and Her Majesty should be with you in about thirty-five minutes from now."

36

The Ethics Wing had been beautifully opened. All the right questions had been asked, all the right sentiments expressed. Among the wives sipping champagne in the Refreshments Extension afterwards the talk was of nothing but Nobbs.

"She didn't look *anything* like her photographs."

"She looked as if she had a sort of beard to me."

"Oh, it wasn't the Queen."

"Wasn't it?"

"They say it was a young man from the Institute here."

"*Really?*"

"Very bravely standing in at the last moment because the Queen couldn't get here."

"Well, I think he was marvellous."

"So natural."

"And human."

"Not at all stuck up."

"Absolutely *marvellous*."

"You felt you could talk to him, somehow, didn't you?"

"Oh, he had a word for everyone. Did you notice?"

"He said, 'So pleased to meet you' to the woman standing next but one to me. Well, I could have *died*."

"Do you know what he said to me?"

"No?"

"He said: 'Bloody hell.'"

"*No!*"

"Isn't it marvellous?"

"So natural and uninhibited."

"So refreshingly un-stuffed-shirt."

"I think he's *marvellous*."

Nobbs was indeed looking radiant. In between celebratory

glasses of champagne he kept nudging Chiddingfold in the ribs and asking merrily:

"How was that then, eh?"

Chiddingfold kept his frozen smile going, restored by the success of the occasion to his normal level of unease. Nunn was in great form, signalling perpetually for the waiter to bring more champagne. He even remembered Zinnia, and sent a waiter to fetch her from the switchboard to join in the celebrations.

"No calls?" he asked.

"Just the one you took, Mr. Nunn."

"Jolly good."

Nothing since the call from the airport. It was extraordinarily jolly good luck that it had not occurred to Goldwasser to use the phone. Now that Zinnia was out here, of course, Goldwasser could phone away to his heart's content. Nunn had a vague impression that he could hear a distant banging and shouting, but it was scarcely audible over the noise of the celebration. Banging and shouting indeed! It struck Nunn that he had perhaps overestimated the intelligence of his adversary. Not a very bright man, Goldwasser, after all.

Riddle was looking for Goldwasser.

"Why, isn't he here?" asked Rowe.

"I can't see him. I thought he was missing earlier on."

"Oh, he'll be around somewhere," said Macintosh.

"I couldn't see him at the hand-shaking."

"Oh, I think I saw him," said Macintosh.

"I'm sure I did, too," said Haugh.

"I think I saw him at the tape-cutting," said Rowe.

"So did I," said Haugh.

"He's around somewhere," said Macintosh.

Nobbs, who had started throwing his empty champagne glasses over his shoulder, was now shaking more hands. He shook Mr. and Mrs. Chiddingfold's hands, and Mr. and Mrs. Vulgurian's, and Mrs. Plushkov's.

"Pleased to meet you," he said. "Most interesting. I'm very glad to see the work you're doing here. How very interesting."

166

A stream of people kept coming up to Mrs. Plushkov and congratulating her on her organisation, and especially on finding Nobbs to play the Queen.

"I believe your husband is here," they all said. "I do so hope you'll introduce us. We've all wanted to meet him for such a long time."

"He's here somewhere," Mrs. Plushkov would say. "I'm not sure exactly where at the moment."

Macintosh had taken Rowe to one side.

"Yes," Rowe was saying. "Yes."

"I mean, you could get it done faster by programming a computer to do it."

"Yes. Y-e-e-e-s."

"There's nothing inherently impossible about programming a computer to write a novel."

"No. Oh, no."

"We could programme Echo IV, the new computer they've parked in the Ethics Wing, to do the job, very easily. Not a very profound or original novel at this stage, perhaps. Not a very good one. Not the complex, sophisticated sort of thing that you're probably producing. But a novel none the less."

"Y-e-e-e-s," said Rowe.

Nunn had the waiters bring out the case of whisky he had laid up for a private tot or two after the Queen's departure. He was getting on very well with Vulgurian, who was leaning informally on the back of Sir Prestwick Wining's wheelchair and telling Nunn all about the programmes Amalgamated Television produced.

"We don't despise popularity," he was saying. "We're not ashamed that 'It's a Giggle' is—where is 'It's a Giggle' in the charts at the moment, Prestwick?"

"Tied fourth with 'Quids In,' R.V.," said Sir Prestwick, who was sipping weakly at a glucose drink, and spoke with a certain effort.

"Jolly good," said Nunn.

"But we're also proud and privileged to present our weekly

intellectual programme, called—what's our intellectual show called, Prestwick?"

"'Athens of the North,' R.V."

"It's a topical discussion programme in classical Greek. No one watches it—almost literally no one at all. What are the ratings, Prestwick?"

"Too small to measure, R.V."

"And yet we shouldn't dream of taking it off."

"Jolly good."

"Proud and privileged."

"A little more whisky, Mr. Vulgurian?" suggested Nunn.

"Thank you. Proud and privileged. No, as I was saying—what's that banging, Prestwick?"

Nobbs had started out round the room to shake everybody's hand.

"Most pleased," he was saying. "Charmed to meet you. Delighted to make your acquaintance."

"Isn't he *marvellous*?" said all the wives all over again. "So absolutely at home with everyone."

One or two of the younger people from the less conventional departments started to dance. Riddle had disappeared. Haugh was agreeing with the sales director of the flooring company that without any doubt whatsoever the world had been created between the 8th and the 14th of July, 5663 B.C. Vulgurian had put his arm round Chiddingfold's shoulder.

"We're proud and privileged to produce 'It's a Giggle,' Mr. Chiddingfold. Proud and privileged."

"Another spot of whisky?" said Nunn.

"Proud and privileged. Just a thumblefill, Ken, just a weeny thumblefill. Proud and—for God's sake, Prestwick, get something done about that infernal banging!"

The world around Nunn seemed very warm and merry and familiar. It took him back to the old days, when after a vigorous day's exercise extracting information from some recalcitrant native he would come back full of modest triumph to a jolly good booze-up of one sort or another in the mess. What were the games they used to play? Indoor rugby. British bulldogs. "Where Art Thou, Moriarty?" All jolly good games. He picked up an empty whisky bottle and looked round for someone to pass it to.

"Come along, then!" he shouted. "Let's have you!"

But no one took much notice, and in the end he did a fast low pass to a man who wasn't looking just to teach him for being such a rotten sport.

"Come along, then!" he called, but the man began to shout and rub his knee and hop about. A knot of people collected round him sympathising. Nunn could see the rugby bottle on the floor in the middle of the group, and scented battle. He bent double and plunged in, throwing his arms round the waists of the two people on either side and shouting: "Heel! Heel, damn you!"

More and more people were dancing. Nobbs had started on his rounds all over again, this time shaking everyone's left hand, to remove any possible suspicion that he was too conventional or supercilious to extend the royal largesse to left hands.

"He's got such a sense of fun," said the wives, as they helped to hold him upright with their right hands. "Honestly, I think he's *wonderful*."

Vulgurian was leaning heavily on Chiddingfold's shoulder, and squeezing Mrs. Chiddingfold's arm.

"Husband put on a wonderful show," he was telling her. "Proud and privileged to be here. Went off with no hags or snitches. No hags or snitches? What do I mean, Prestwick?"

"No snigs or hatches, R.V.," said Sir Prestwick, whose face looked remarkably grey and drawn.

Nunn had extracted himself from the scrum, and was leading a party of laboratory technicians in throwing crab sandwiches and empty liquor bottles at the two reporters and a photographer trapped inside the Press enclosure.

Jellicoe came in and plucked Nunn's sleeve.

"I beg your pardon, sir," he said. "But there's another

contingent of the upper classes arriving in a kind of funeral cortège of Rolls-Royces and Daimlers."

"Jolly good," said Nunn. "Send 'em across. Any chums of yours are chums of mine."

Into the Refreshments Extension from the direction of the Political Department came Riddle, pink-cheeked and bright-eyed, and leading a battered little man with round shoulders and a patient, embarrassed smile.

"I want you to meet Mr. Plushkov," she said loudly to everyone within earshot. "We're going to be married."

37

"Echo IV," wrote Echo IV, far away in the calm remoteness of the Rothermere Vulgurian Ethics Wing, "is a brilliant new arrival on the literary scene. *The Tin Men* is its first novel, and critics who have seen it prior to publication . . ."

Also by Michael Frayn

The Russian Interpreter

'A love affair through an interpreter,' said Raya. 'That's a very cultured prospect.'

Raya is a mercurial Moscow blonde who speaks no English, and the affair she is embarking upon is with Gordon Proctor-Gould, a visiting English businessman who speaks no Russian. They need an interpreter, which is how Paul Manning is diverted from writing his thesis at Moscow University, to be drawn deeper and deeper into all the deceptions of love and East–West relations.

'A little masterpiece.' FINANCIAL TIMES

'Imaginative and delightful – characters who stick in the memory and have a genuine life of their own. Frayn juxtaposes the humorous and the frankly sinister into a satisfying and witty picture.' SUNDAY TELEGRAPH

'Frayn . . . has been compared to Wodehouse, but here it is Waugh to the knife.' GUARDIAN

ff

Sweet Dreams

Heaven, reported St John in Revelation, was a cubical city 12,000 furlongs high made of 'pure gold, like unto clear glass'. That was 1,900 years ago, and Heaven today has changed out of all recognition. So discovers Howard Baker, who, after a car accident on earth, finds a celestial metropolis which offers rich opportunities for leisure and enjoyment – but one which also presents a moral and intellectual challenge for the likes of modest, responsible, likeable, educated men such as Howard.

'A small masterpiece.' Christopher Hudson, NEW SOCIETY

'Lucid, intelligent, delightful, stylish, extremely funny . . . I recommend it wholeheartedly.' Margaret Drabble, NEW YORK TIMES

'An impeccable writer. He is not a science fictionist but a moralist, and his novel is a kind of *Candide* – a vividly contemporary *Candide*, full of the most serious high comedy and the most enormous belly laughs.' NEW YORKER

ff

A Very Private Life

Uncumber lives at a time in the distant future when all humanity is divided in two – the Insiders and the Outsiders. The Insiders are privileged, with their every need catered to by somatic drugs, three-dimensional holovision and a prolonged life. Uncumber lives in this luxurious world and is told that she must never go out into the dust and disease of the real world, but she is haunted by a restless and inquisitive spirit. When she falls in love with an Outsider, she decides to go exploring . . .

'A fairy tale of the future.' GUARDIAN

'Easily the most original thing Frayn has done . . . written with elegant simplicity.' NEW STATESMAN

'An ingenious fable . . . at times poetically imaginative.' SUNDAY TIMES

Skios

Arriving on the Greek island of Skios to spend a few stolen summer days with someone else's girlfriend, Oliver Fox discovers that she's missed her flights, and that he has twenty-four long hours to kill by himself. In the arrivals hall, he sees the name 'Dr Norman Wilfred' being held up. It's a temptingly possible substitute – so Oliver steps into the life of Dr Wilfred.

On the same flight is the real Dr Wilfred, who has come to give a lecture to a distinguished international audience. By the time the wrong Dr Wilfred is on his way to give the right Dr Wilfred's lecture, and the right Dr Wilfred is installed in the wrong Dr Wilfred's love nest, Oliver's original date has found a flight after all and is stepping off a plane herself . . .

'This book risks being unreadable . . . tears of laughter make the print swim in front of your eyes.' Peter Kemp, SUNDAY TIMES

'A transfixingly witty novel about riding one's luck and being undone by it.' FINANCIAL TIMES

'It's unlikely that there'll be another book this year that will make you laugh as much as this one does; a writer has to be very smart to write something so sublimely silly.' METRO

ff

Headlong

**Shortlisted for the Booker Prize, the Whitbread Novel Award
and the James Tait Memorial Prize for Fiction**

Martin Clay, a would-be art historian, believes he has discovered a
missing masterpiece. The owner of the painting is oblivious to its
potential and asks Martin to help him sell it, leaving Martin with
the chance of a lifetime: if he can only separate the painting from
its owner, he would be able to perform a great public service, to
make his professional reputation – perhaps make rather a lot of
money as well. But is the painting really what Martin believes it
to be? As Martin is drawn further into this moral and intellectual
labyrinth, events start to spiral out of his control . . .

'A knife-edge thriller/farce about a missing Bruegel masterpiece
and its rightful custodians.' INDEPENDENT

'Frayn's plot – a high-precision feat of fictional engineering –
accelerates exhilaratingly . . . a black and brilliant comedy of
uncertainties.' SUNDAY TIMES

'Ingenious . . . As entertaining as it is intelligent, as stimulating as
it is funny.' NEW YORK TIMES

Spies

Winner of the Whitbread Novel of the Year Award

In the quiet cul-de-sac where Keith and Stephen live the only immediate signs of the Second World War are the blackout at night and a single random bombsite. But the two boys start to suspect all is not as it seems when one day Keith announces a disconcerting discovery: the Germans have infiltrated his own family. And when the secret underground world they have dreamed up emerges from the shadows, they find themselves engulfed in mysteries far deeper and more painful than they had bargained for.

'A beautifully accomplished, richly nostalgic novel about supposed second-world-war espionage seen through the eyes of a young boy.' SUNDAY TIMES

'A novel with a vivid sympathy for how lonely, scared and helpless being a child often feels, and how easily and eagerly we forget it . . . A pleasure to read.' GUARDIAN

'This brilliant and serious novel is Frayn on absolutely top – if unashamedly smart – form.' DAILY TELEGRAPH

ff

Towards the End of the Morning

Michael Frayn's classic novel is set in the crossword and nature notes department of an obscure national newspaper during the declining years of Fleet Street. John Dyson, a mid-level editor, dreams wistfully of fame and the gentlemanly life – until one day his great chance of glory arrives. But does he have what it takes to succeed in the exciting world of television?

'Still ranks with Evelyn Waugh's *Scoop* as one of the funniest novels about journalists ever written.' SUNDAY TIMES

'A sublimely funny comedy about the ways newspapers try to put lives into words.' SPECTATOR

'*Towards the End of the Morning* certainly keeps you laughing, but the jokes illuminate the characters and their destinies with a clarity that makes you miss a heartbeat after the laughs.' THE TIMES